WAY OF THE WARRIOR KID

WAY OF THE
WARRIOR
KID

**FROM WIMPY
TO WARRIOR
THE NAVY SEAL WAY**

JOCKO WILLINK

ILLUSTRATED BY **JON BOZAK**

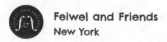
Feiwel and Friends
New York

A Feiwel and Friends Book

An imprint of Macmillan Publishing Group, LLC

175 Fifth Avenue, New York, NY 10010

Our books may be purchased in bulk for promotional, educational, or business use. Please contact your local bookseller or the Macmillan Corporate and Premium Sales Department at (800) 221-7945 ext. 5442 or by e-mail at MacmillanSpecialMarkets@macmillan.com.

Library of Congress Control Number: 2017931717

ISBN 978-1-250-15107-0 (hardcover) / ISBN 978-1-250-15106-3 (ebook)

Book design by Liz Dresner

Feiwel and Friends logo designed by Filomena Tuosto

First Edition—2017

20 19 18 17 16 15

mackids.com

This book is dedicated to
Marc Lee, Mike Monsoor, and Ryan Job,
from SEAL Team Three, Task Unit Bruiser,
who lived, and fought, and died
as warriors.

CHAPTER 1: THE WORST YEAR

Tomorrow is the last day of school, and I CAN'T WAIT FOR IT TO BE OVER!! This has been the worst year EVER! The bad part is that I don't see how next year is going to be any better at all. Fifth grade was horrible—I'm afraid sixth grade will be EVEN WORSE. Why was it so bad? Where do I begin?

This is ME (Marc).

I'm the hot dog-eating champ in my house!

This guy can beat me in a foot race.

Top five reasons why fifth grade was HORRIBLE:

1. It's school! I'm sitting at a desk ALL DAY.
2. I learned that I'm dumb! That's right. All the other grades I thought I was "smart." But this year was a FAILURE! I still don't know my times tables! How the heck am I going to make it through next year?

$$0 \times 0 =$$

3. School lunches. They call it "pizza." I have no idea why. Since when does a piece of white bread count as pizza crust???????

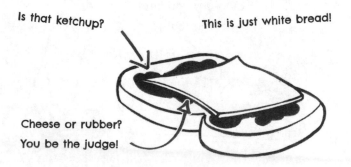

Is that ketchup?

This is just white bread!

Cheese or rubber?
You be the judge!

4. Gym class. Most people like gym. But at my school we have "tests" and I completely stink. Especially at PULL-UPS. Guess how many pull-ups I can do? ZERO! I can do ZERO pull-ups! I'm a disgrace to ten-year-olds—and the whole class knows it. Even the girls. Especially the girls that can do more pull-ups than me!!

I did one pull-up. How many can you do?

I try not to define my efforts with numbers.

5. Field trips. Just like gym class, most kids like field trips. Well, we go to one place for field trips: Mount Tom. We go there in the fall before it gets too cold and in the spring when it starts to get warm. But here's the thing: Mount Tom isn't a mountain. It's a lake. Here's the problem: I CAN'T SWIM! I hid it pretty well during our fall trip. But this spring,

kids noticed. "Why don't you come out in the water?" "Why are you staying on the beach?" "Why don't you jump off the diving board?" What kind of person can't even swim? ME: That's what kind of person! AAAHHH!

6. I know I said top five reasons, but there is one more, and it's probably the biggest reason: Kenny Williamson. He is big and he is MEAN. He rules the jungle gym. He even calls himself "King of the Jungle Gym" or "King Kenny"!! If any other kids want to play on the jungle gym, they either have to be friends with Kenny or follow his "rules."

These things could hurt someone!

A HUMAN TIME BOMB!

All the teachers talk about how my school is "bully-free." We even had a No Bully Day, where we talked about bullying and how bad it was and how we should tell the teachers if we saw it happening. Well, let me tell you, Kenny is definitely a BULLY, and he definitely is in my school. And no one says anything to the teachers about it!

Those are the top reasons that fifth grade was horrible, and sixth grade isn't going to be much better! I can't wait for school to be over tomorrow so the suffering can STOP and summer can START!

This summer is going to be AWESOME. Yes, it is cool that I won't have to be in school—but something even cooler is happening. My uncle Jake is coming to stay with us for the whole summer!

He has been a Navy SEAL for eight years and is getting out of the Navy to go to college. Before he goes to college, he is going to stay with us the whole summer long. A Navy SEAL! FOR REAL. IN MY HOUSE!!!!!

Uncle Jake is the best. First, he is super cool because he is a Navy SEAL. He fought in real wars. My mom says he was "on the front lines." That means he was face-to-face with the bad guys. Whoa! Uncle Jake is also awesome because he is the COMPLETE OPPOSITE OF ME. I am weak—he is strong. I am dumb—he is smart. I can't swim—he can swim with a backpack on! I'm scared of bullies—bullies are scared of him!

MY UNCLE JAKE!!

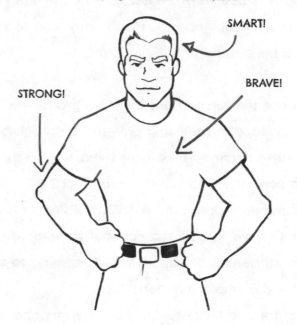

SMART!

BRAVE!

STRONG!

Anyway, I haven't spent too much time with Uncle Jake because we live in California, and he has been stationed in Virginia for a long time. I hope he doesn't think I'm such a DUMB WIMP that he won't even hang around with me! Maybe he won't notice?

AAHHHHH!!! Of course he will. He is a tough guy! I'm a dork! Well, I guess I will find out soon.

CHAPTER 2: THE WORST DAY

Today was the absolute worst day OF MY LIFE. I know the last day of school is SUPPOSED to be fun, but let me tell you, it was miserable, horrible, awful, and terrible. How can that be? Where do I start?

First, it was Sports Day, which is SUPPOSED to be fun. It means we are out at the recess area all morning playing a bunch of games and challenges and stuff. Not just stuff like soccer and basketball but also things like three-legged races, bobbing for apples, and potato-sack races. We would do each activity for a while until we were told to "rotate" by the teachers, and then we would go on to the next activity. At first it wasn't so bad. No one was taking it that seriously, and everyone was just kind of having fun.

That meant no one really noticed how LAME I was at all these different sports and games. Especially because Fred Turner was in my group, and he is even worse than I am at everything. So it wasn't too bad.

First time in a sack race, Fred?

UNTIL PULL-UP TIME. That's right. One of the activities we were doing was pull-ups and push-ups and stuff on the jungle gym. WITH EVERYONE WATCHING! So I did what any smart, weak kid would do: I HID! I went to the back of the line and just kind of blended in. When the other kids would jump on the pull-up bar, everyone would count for them. Mike Swearington did eighteen. Billy Hacker did twenty-two! Jennifer Phillips, who does gymnastics, did twenty-seven!

There I was, standing in the back watching, hiding, and waiting for this to end.

Then, it was King of the Jungle Gym Kenny Williamson's turn. He went up and did eleven, which is actually pretty good when you consider how HUGE he is. He didn't seem to care, until someone yelled from the crowd, "He's not as strong as he looks!" There was some laughter, and I saw Kenny getting madder and madder. He wasn't sure what to do until he saw me looking at him, and our eyes locked.

He slowly raised his finger and pointed it straight at me.

"What about him?" Kenny barked. The crowd suddenly got quiet as Kenny stood pointing at me.

"He hasn't gone yet! Let's see what Marc can do!" This was pure evil. Kenny knew very well that I couldn't do any pull-ups. He had seen me in gym class trying to do one for the last year and failing every time. I shrank farther back into the crowd. "Come on, Marc! Get on up here!" Kenny yelled.

At that moment, someone shoved me from behind, forcing me out of the pack and into the open. I couldn't hide anymore.

Mr. Maguire, the teacher in charge of this activity, turned and looked at me. "Have you gone yet, Marc?" he asked.

"No, Mr. Maguire. But I'm . . ." I tried to think of some kind of an excuse. I'm sick? But I just did all the other games. I got hurt? But how could I get hurt watching people do pull-ups? The dog ate my pull-ups?

"Then jump on up there, Marc," said Mr. Maguire with a stern but encouraging look. "Let's see what you've got."

"Okay," I said. I slowly made my way to the pull-up bar. The entire crowd was staring right at me. All I saw were eyes everywhere.

"Go ahead, Marc. Get up there," said Mr. Maguire.

"Yeah," shouted Kenny. "Let's see what you got!"

I finally got to the pull-up bar and looked up at it. I wished so hard that this one time I could do some pull-ups. Or that I could just disappear. "Come on, Marc, let's go," said Mr. Maguire.

I wonder if that bar knows it's about to ruin my life.

"Yeah, Marc, *let's go*," added Kenny, mocking Mr. Maguire.

The crowd became completely quiet as I reached up. I bent my legs, jumped up, and grabbed the bar. I hung there. I started to pull. Nothing happened. I pulled harder. Nothing happened. I wiggled my body around. Nothing happened. Finally, with all my might, I pulled as hard as I have ever pulled anything in my entire life. I went up about two inches, then stopped. I pulled more but didn't move any higher. Slowly, gravity brought me back down. I dropped off the bar.

"ZERO!!!!!!" Kenny yelled at the top of his lungs. "A. BIG. FAT. ZERO."

The crowd joined in: "Zero! Zero! Zero! Zero!"

I hung my head and tried to become invisible.

"All right, all right," Mr.

Maguire said, trying to quiet the crowd. "Not everyone can do a pull-up."

Then, from the back of the crowd, someone blurted out, "He can't swim, either!" Everyone laughed. Even though I know that not being able to do pull-ups and not being able to swim don't make you a bad person, I had had enough. I could feel tears building up in my eyes. I didn't want anyone to see me cry, so I ran. I ran off the recess field, through the courtyard, and behind the library, where no one ever goes. I sat down, and that was it. I cried like a little baby.

That was my last day of school.

CHAPTER 3: THE BEGINNING OF SUMMER

"What's wrong?" my mom asked as I sat at the table eating breakfast. After yesterday, it was hard to even PRETEND to be happy. I tried.

"Nothing. I'm fine," I told her with a forced smile.

"Come on, Marc. What's bothering you?" That is the thing with my mom. She understands enough to know that I'm not happy, but even if I told her what was wrong, what could she do about it? She couldn't make me stronger. She couldn't make Kenny Williamson leave me alone. So what is the point in telling her what was wrong? If I did, she would say something like, "Well, that boy is just jealous because you are smarter than he is," or "You'll get stronger when you get a little older," or "Don't worry about what other people say, because I know how very special you are."

My mom really loves me.

While I know that my mom means well here, the fact of the matter is Kenny Williamson *is not* jealous of me. It doesn't matter if I get stronger when I'm older, I'm weak *now*!!!!! And of course my *mom* thinks I'm special—she's my *MOM*! So seriously, there was no point in telling my mom what was *really* wrong.

"I'm just going to miss my friends over the summer," I told her.

"Awwwwww," she answered. "Well, we can make sure you get to play with them a lot this summer."

"Thanks, Mom," I told her, hoping that she would just leave me alone. My mom is really nice, but she works a ton and is always at her office, and a lot of the time it seems she just doesn't really understand me. That's okay. I know she is trying to be nice. My dad is nice, too, but he is gone most of the time, traveling for his job and stuff.

"I'll tell you what," she added, "your uncle Jake arrives in about an hour. Do you want to come pick him up with me?"

"YES!" I shouted. I had forgotten the exact day that Uncle Jake was supposed to get here, but now I remembered it was today! "Yes! That's great."

"Okay, then," she said. "Clear the table and we'll head out."

Guess who's psyched
to see Uncle Jake?

After I cleaned up the table, we got into the car
and headed to the airport. I was excited about Uncle
Jake coming, but I was also kinda nervous. He's a Navy
SEAL—an official tough guy. And not tough like the guys
in the movies that just *act* tough—Uncle Jake is the
real deal. So, even though he probably won't want to
hang around with me much, at least I will get to see
him a little.

At the airport, we parked the car and headed to
the terminal to pick him up.

I stood there looking through the glass at the
passengers coming down the hallway. There were
families, businessmen, college students, and a bunch
of other regular-looking people arriving and walking
from their planes. Then I saw him. He was walking at a
steady pace, right toward us.

He seemed to know where he was going. He had a very serious look on his face. He looked STRONG. He was wearing a short-sleeved shirt, and his arms were big! While all the other people seemed to be thinking about themselves, Uncle Jake was slowly looking around, scanning the whole area. Then he saw my mom and me. His head locked on our position. We waved.

Suddenly, his serious face cracked, he let out a big smile, and he waved back to us. AWESOME! He walked through the door and came over to us. He hugged my mom and said, "How ya doin', big sister?" which was funny because he was A LOT bigger than she was. Then he looked at me, held out his hand, and said, "Little man?" I shook his hand. His hand was different. It was big and strong and rough—it felt like leather more than skin. "Is that all ya got?" he said.

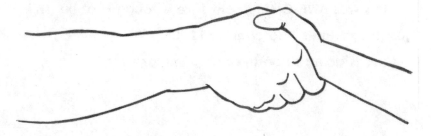

"What?" I replied, not entirely sure what he was talking about.

"That handshake. Is that as hard as you can squeeze?"

I squeezed harder.

"Better," said Uncle Jake. "We'll work on that."

"Okay," I replied. COOL! *We* were going to *work on that*. That means we were going to work together. So I guess we will do some stuff together! We made our way over to the baggage claim so Uncle Jake could get his bags. He had one green army backpack on and another camouflage duffel bag. He threw the duffel bag at the ground in front of me.

"You carry that—it will make you stronger," he said with a smile on his face.

"No problem," I told him, happy to be able to carry a really cool-looking army bag. I picked it up—it was heavy—and put it over my shoulder. We started to walk back to the car.

This was AWESOME. Uncle Jake is tough—but he isn't just tough. He is also cool and NICE.

This is going to be the best summer ever.

CHAPTER 4: ROOMMATES

Well, today was awesome and then terrible and then, I think, awesome again. When we got home, I realized Uncle Jake was staying in my room! We were going to be roommates for the whole summer. My mom has a little fold-out guest bed that she put in my room for me. The mattress is thin and kind of uncomfortable, but I don't care. Uncle Jake is using my bed for the summer. So we got all that figured out, and Uncle Jake put his stuff in some of my drawers and some other stuff in my closet. Then we went down and ate dinner.

During dinner, my mom asked Uncle Jake a bunch of questions about everything. He has been in the SEAL Teams for eight years, and he told her about a bunch of the cool things he has done. They are all things that any kid would love to do, like parachuting, scuba diving, rappelling out of helicopters, and blowing things up with explosives—

all the time!

He also talked about being in war. He said the hard part wasn't the missions or carrying all that gear or being afraid—he said the hard parts were the times when his friends got hurt or killed.

After dinner, we went upstairs to go "square away" (that's an Uncle Jake term!) my room before it got too late. This is when things got BAD.

Uncle Jake asked me what I was doing the next day. "Are you going to meet with some of your friends? Go play some basketball or soccer or something?"

"I'm not that great at sports," I told him.

My World-Famous
Basketball "Moves"

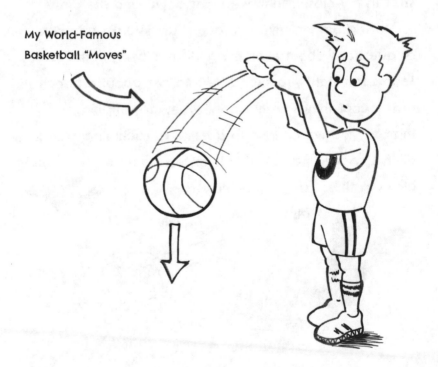

"You don't have to be good to have fun."

"Well, it's not really that fun when you aren't good," I answered, already feeling like a big wimp.

"Okay. How about a swim? There has got to be someplace to go swimming around here, right?"

When he said that, I suddenly felt terrible. Here I was with my own uncle who wants to go swimming with me, but I can't because I don't even know how to swim! I felt like I didn't even deserve him as an uncle. Tears suddenly welled up in my eyes, and I blurted out, "I can't swim."

"What do you mean you can't swim?" he asked.

"I mean I can't swim."

"At all?" he questioned me.

"At all. I can't swim at all." As I said that, I finally just burst. Tears came streaming out of my eyes. Then I told him everything that I didn't tell my mom. *Everything.* "Not only that, but I can't do any pull-ups. I'm probably the weakest kid in the school." The tears really started coming down now. Even though I was looking like a complete baby, I couldn't stop myself from crying or talking. "And it's not just that. I don't know my times tables yet! I'm almost eleven years old, and I don't know my times tables!!!!"

"Okay, you know there's—" Uncle Jake was trying to tell me something, but I cut him off. I can't believe it, but I butted right in and started talking over him.

"And the worst part is, I get bullied. Almost every day I have to do what Kenny Williamson tells me to do!!"

"Who's Kenny Williamson?" asked Uncle Jake. "A teacher?"

"No!" I shouted. "He's another kid. A bully!"

"All right, I get it," Uncle Jake said. "Is that it?"

"Is that it???? I get picked on by a bully, made fun of because I can't do any pull-ups, I don't know what eight times seven is, and I don't even know how to swim!! How much worse can it get???" I said loudly.

"Good," said Uncle Jake.

"Good?" I asked. "How the heck is all that good?"

"It's good because every one of those problems is something you can change. Every one of them."

I didn't know what to say. Here I was, a complete mess, crying over my situation. But Uncle Jake was calm, so calm it made me start to get calm, too.

"Look, Marc," he said, "when I joined the Navy, I could only do seven pull-ups. Now I can do forty-seven. I wasn't a great swimmer. Now I can swim like a fish. I also didn't do that well in school, but when I got into SEAL training, I learned how to learn and ended up doing great on all the academic tests. And finally, when I first got into the SEAL Teams, I knew nothing about fighting. But now I can handle myself in any situation."

"Of course you can! You're a Navy SEAL!"

"You are missing the point. I wasn't born like this! I had to work for it. I had to learn it. I had to EARN it. And what I am telling you is that instead of being a wimpy kid, you can be a Warrior Kid."

WARRIOR KID??!?!?! I wasn't exactly sure what that really meant, but it sounded AWESOME.

"What is a Warrior Kid?" I asked.

"I'll tell you about it tomorrow. You need to go to bed. But I think a Warrior Kid is exactly what you need to become."

Uncle Jake walked out the door to go downstairs and talk to my mom. WARRIOR KID. WARRIOR KID. WOW.

I lay on my mattress thinking about this as I drifted off to sleep. . . .

CHAPTER 5: WARRIOR KID

When I woke up the next morning, Uncle Jake wasn't in my room anymore. I didn't know where he was. I walked downstairs. He was at the breakfast table with my mom.

"What's up, sleepy?" he said. I rubbed my eyes. He was right; I was still sleepy.

"What have you been doing?" I asked.

"Well," he replied, "I woke up, worked out, went for a run, took a shower, reviewed some reading that was recommended for college, and now I'm having breakfast with my sister."

"You did all that this morning?"

"I sure did."

"What time did you wake up?"

"Zero-dark-thirty," Uncle Jake replied.

"What the heck is that?" I asked.

Uncle Jake smiled. "That means I get up early. Very early."

I had no idea anyone could wake up that early. I have a hard time getting out of bed by seven to get ready for school. Uncle Jake must have gotten up around five!

"You and I need to talk today, don't we?"

"Yes, we do," I replied anxiously.

"All right, then. Finish your breakfast, and we'll go for a walk."

I scarfed down some food, threw on my clothes, and told Uncle Jake I was ready.

"You sure you're ready?" he asked with a serious look on his face.

"I'm pretty sure," I told him even though I felt nervous.

"All right, then," he told me. "Let's go."

We headed out the door and down the street toward the park.

"So, Marc, what do you know about being a

warrior?" Uncle Jake asked me as soon as we turned the first corner.

"I don't think I know anything about being a warrior," I told him.

"Okay. Well, then do you even know what a warrior is?"

"Yes. I mean I guess I know. A warrior is someone who fights in wars . . . right?"

"That is one part of it. But what else?"

"I'm not sure what else."

"So do you think that the only way to be a warrior is to fight in wars? And do you think that anyone who fights in a war is a warrior?"

"I guess so," I answered.

Guess who has no idea
what he's talking about?

"Well, you guessed wrong. There is a lot more to being a warrior than just being in a war. Warriors are people that stand up for themselves. They face challenges. Warriors work hard to achieve goals. They have the discipline to overcome their weaknesses. Warriors are people that constantly try to test and improve themselves. And yes, war is the ultimate test, but not all warriors go to war."

"But how can a kid be a warrior?" I asked. It just didn't seem like a kid would be able to do all those things that Uncle Jake was talking about.

I'm the warrior of sleeping.

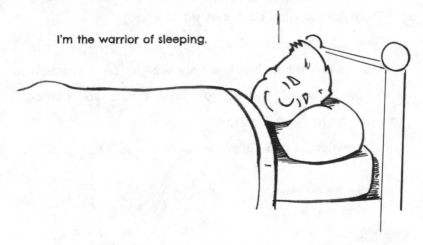

"By doing everything I just said. A normal kid doesn't push himself—a Warrior Kid does. A normal kid doesn't work constantly to improve himself—a Warrior Kid does. I look at all these problems you cried to me about yesterday. A Warrior Kid wouldn't cry about those problems. A Warrior Kid would *do* something about those problems."

"Do what?"

"Do what? Do whatever it takes. Every problem you have can be overcome. EVERY ONE OF THEM. You can't do pull-ups? You work out and get stronger until you can. You don't know your times tables? You study and train your mind until you know them cold. You can't swim? You learn how. You get picked on? You learn to fight."

"Fight?" I asked.

"Yes, fight. Just like anything else in the world, there are techniques to fighting—like learning a sport—and when you know the techniques and practice them, you can defend yourself from anyone."

"You really think I could do all that?"

"I know you can. Like I told you last night, I had to transform myself when I got into the Navy. I had to get stronger. I had to learn to fight. I even had to learn to learn. But I did it. And if I did it, so can you. Do you want to? Do you want to overcome all these challenges you face?"

"Of course!" I shouted, feeling pretty fired up about everything Uncle Jake was telling me. "Who wouldn't?"

Then Uncle Jake got really serious. Anything resembling a smile left his face. He looked me straight in the eyes and said, "But let me tell you something. This will not be easy. This will be harder than anything you've ever done before. I will help you, but you are the one that has to do the work. You have to want the change. That has to come from you. Do you want to do this?"

I was a little nervous after what he just said, but the thought of overcoming so many problems was like an explosion in my head. "Yes, I do."

"I need a commitment because I don't want to waste my time on you. Do you promise?" Uncle Jake asked as he held out his hand for a shake.

I felt the most pressure I have ever felt in my life. I looked him in the eyes and said, "Yes. I promise." We shook hands.

"We start tomorrow morning," Uncle Jake said quietly.

We walked through the park and back to the house without saying another word.

Something had already changed.

CHAPTER 6: THE PROGRAM BEGINS

OH, WOW! Today was just crazy—and I mean CRAZY! I was sound asleep in my bed this morning, peacefully dreaming about a double cheeseburger with fries and a milk shake from my favorite restaurant, the Classic Malt Shoppe.

So there I was, enjoying this lovely dream. The food had been delivered and was sitting in front of me, and I was just about to take my first bite of that delicious double cheeseburger when—*CLANG! CLANG! CLANG! CLANG!* A shocking noise scared me half to death. My heart nearly jumped out of my chest. I thought I was being attacked by aliens from outer space who used broken, old drum cymbals as their main weapon!

Then I heard the voice of one of the alien monsters yelling at me, "GET OUT OF BED!" I immediately thought that this alien sounded an awful lot like Uncle Jake. Yep, you guessed it—that was because it WAS Uncle Jake. He had a broomstick and a metal garbage can, and he was banging them together and yelling at me to get out of bed and give him fifty push-ups. Still confused and thinking about the double cheeseburger I was about to dig into in my dream, I told the alien that I didn't think I could do five push-ups, so fifty was out of the question.

But Uncle Jake didn't care at all about my cheeseburger or how many push-ups I could do. He put the garbage can next to my head and banged EVEN LOUDER! I rolled out of bed and did nine push-ups before I fell flat on my face.

When I finally looked around, I realized that it was STILL DARK OUTSIDE! I asked Uncle Jake what time it was, and he said it was time to get up and get busy!!!

That is how my day started. From there Uncle Jake showed me a bunch of exercises—and then made me do them. The weird thing was that all these exercises had strange names that seemed to put a big smile on Uncle Jake's face. "Star jumpers." "Burpees." "Diamond push-ups." "Dive-bomber push-ups." "Supermans." "Jackknives." "Belly busters." And let me tell you, even though these names sound funny, THERE WAS NOTHING FUNNY ABOUT THEM AT ALL. They hurt! But Uncle Jake seemed to do them all so easily. Then Uncle Jake gave me a test. I had to do as many squats, push-ups, and sit-ups as I could in two minutes with one minute of rest in between. I did twenty-three squats, fourteen push-ups, and eighteen sit-ups. Then Uncle Jake did the same thing. He did 104 squats, 108 push-ups, and 122 sit-ups!!!!!

I told Uncle Jake I was a WEAKLING! Then he explained to me that I was only weak right now because I had never trained before—never worked out. "In order to make your body strong," he said, "you have to make it work." Then he told me that it all started by getting up early in the morning and "GETTING AFTER IT." I asked if maybe, instead of waking up *so early* we could just do our workout a little later in the day, perhaps at a more REASONABLE time.

Uncle Jake said NO WAY. He said that pushing yourself began every day with PULLING YOURSELF OUT OF BED!

I asked him if that meant I had to have a GARBAGE CAN BANGED IN MY EARS every day.

He said no—as long as I was up and out of bed early enough (!!!!!!), there would be no garbage can!

So it was either get out of bed early or have a garbage can banged in my ears!!

I wasn't so sure I liked this program! But I did have to say one thing that surprised me. Doing all those exercises in the morning actually made me feel better all day. I felt awake and good and like I had extra energy. So even though the early wake up and the exercising was kind of rough, I really liked the way it made me feel for the rest of the day. It was worth it!

CHAPTER 7: WHAT IT MEANS TO BE A WARRIOR

After a few days, I actually got used to getting up so early. By the third day, I didn't get the garbage can in my ears anymore—I was actually waking up early on my own every day! Wow. Today, after the morning routine of exercises, Uncle Jake had a pretty serious talk with me.

"So do you think you are a Warrior Kid yet?" he asked.

"I guess I might be," I told him.

"Why do you think you might be?"

"Well, I'm waking up early every day and doing all the exercises you tell me to do."

"Do you think that makes you a warrior?"

"Maybe?" I asked him . . . but deep down I knew there was a lot more.

"Wrong!" Uncle Jake cut me off. "There is a lot more to being a warrior than just waking up early and working out. A LOT MORE. What do you think the most important part of being a warrior is?"

"Fighting the enemy?" I asked, hoping for some good war stories.

"That is important. But it is just part of the job. Guess again," Uncle Jake said.

"Being in the military?"

"Again—that is a warrior's job. But it isn't the most important part of being a warrior. Got any other guesses?"

"No, Uncle Jake. I'm stumped."

"It's the Warrior Code."

"Is that like a secret language?" I asked.

"No," Uncle Jake laughed. "It's not a secret language. It's the rules warriors live by. The standards they hold for themselves and other warriors in their tribe."

"Like laws?" I asked.

"Not really. Laws are what everyone lives by. They keep order. The Warrior Code isn't enforced by police. It is something that you have to hold yourself to. Something that keeps you on the right path in life."

"What is the code, then? What are the rules?"

"Different warrior groups have different codes, depending on their culture, their time, and their society."

"Which one is the best?"

"They are all different. You need to go and look at them yourself. Read through them. Try to understand their different codes. And then come up with your own Warrior Code that you can live by."

"Okay. Where can I find them?"

"I'll give you some of them when we get home."

When we got back to the house, Uncle Jake pulled out an old three-ring binder. He handed it to me and said simply, "Read."

"I will." And I did.

I went up to my room and opened the notebook. It had a bunch of paper in it with different type and different size pages. Some of it was photocopied. Some of it was handwritten. These are some of the Warrior Codes I found inside:

The SEAL Code

- Loyalty to country, team, and teammate
- Serve with honor and integrity on and off the battlefield
- Ready to lead, ready to follow, never quit
- Take responsibility for your actions and the actions of your teammates
- Excel as warriors through discipline and innovation
- Train for war, fight to win, defeat our nation's enemies
- Earn your trident every day

THE VIKING LAWS

- Be brave and aggressive
  - Be direct
  - Grab all opportunities
  - Use varying methods of attack
  - Be versatile and agile
  - Attack one target at a time
  - Don't plan everything in detail
  - Use top-quality weapons

- Be prepared
  - Keep weapons in good condition
  - Keep in shape
  - Find good battle comrades
  - Agree on important points
  - Choose *one* chief

- Be a good merchant
  - Find out what the market needs
  - Do not promise what you can't keep
  - Do not demand overpayment
  - Arrange things so that you can return

- Keep the camp in order
  - Keep things tidy and organized
  - Arrange enjoyable activities that strengthen the group
  - Make sure everybody does useful work
  - Consult all members of the group for advice

THE RANGER CREED

- *Recognizing that I volunteered as a Ranger, fully knowing the hazards of my chosen profession, I will always endeavor to uphold the prestige, honor, and high esprit de corps of my Ranger regiment.*

- *Acknowledging the fact that a Ranger is a more elite soldier, who arrives at the cutting edge of battle by land, sea, or air, I accept the fact that as a ranger, my country expects me to move farther, faster, and fight harder than any other soldier.*

- *Never shall I fail my comrades. I will always keep myself mentally alert, physically strong, and morally straight, and I will shoulder more than my share of the task, whatever it may be, 100 percent and then some.*

- *Gallantly will I show the world that I am a specially selected and well-trained soldier. My courtesy to superior officers,* neatness of dress, and care of equipment shall set the example for others to follow.

- Energetically will I meet the enemies of my country. I shall defeat them on the field of battle for I am better trained and will fight with all my might. Surrender is not a Ranger word. I will never leave a fallen comrade to fall into the hands of the enemy, and under no circumstances will I ever embarrass my country.

- Readily will I display the intestinal fortitude required to fight on to the Ranger objective and complete the mission, though I be the lone survivor.

Rangers Lead The Way!

THE UNITED STATES MARINE CORPS CORE VALUES

Honor: This is the bedrock of our character. It is the quality that empowers Marines to exemplify the ultimate in ethical and moral behavior: to never lie, cheat, or steal; to abide by an uncompromising code of integrity; to respect human dignity; and to have respect and concern for each other. It represents the maturity, dedication, trust, and dependability that commit Marines to act responsibly, be accountable for their actions, fulfill their obligations, and hold others accountable for their actions.

Courage: The heart of our Core Values, courage is the mental, moral, and physical strength ingrained in Marines that sees them through the challenges of combat and the mastery of fear, and to do what is right, to adhere to a higher standard of personal conduct, to lead by example, and to make tough decisions under stress and pressure. It is the inner strength that enables a Marine to take that extra step.

Commitment: This is the spirit of determination and dedication within members of a force of arms that leads to professionalism and mastery of the art of war. It promotes the highest order of discipline for unit and self and is the ingredient that instills dedication to Corps and country 24 hours a day, pride, concern for others, and an unrelenting determination to achieve a standard of excellence in every endeavor. Commitment is the value that establishes the Marine as the warrior and citizen others strive to emulate.

The US Army Warrior Ethos

I will always place the mission first.

I will never accept defeat.

I will never quit.

I will never leave a fallen comrade.

The Seven Virtues of Bushido (Samurai Code)

- Integrity
- Respect
- Heroic courage
- Honor
- Compassion
- Honesty and sincerity
- Duty and loyalty

The Code of Chivalry for
Knights of the Middle Ages

- To fear God and maintain His Church
- To serve the liege lord in valor and faith
- To protect the weak and defenseless
- To give succor to widows and orphans
- To refrain from the wanton giving of offence
- To live by honor and for glory
- To despise pecuniary reward
- To fight for the welfare of all
- To obey those placed in authority
- To guard the honor of fellow knights
- To eschew unfairness, meanness, and deceit
- To keep faith
- At all times to speak the truth
- To persevere to the end in any enterprise begun
- To respect the honor of women
- Never to refuse a challenge from an equal
- Never to turn the back upon a foe

These things were super cool. I knew I had to start thinking about what Uncle Jake said: making a Warrior Code of my own. I started thinking about what it would say and what it would mean to live by a code like this.

CHAPTER 8: A GIFT OF STRENGTH

This morning, I got up when my alarm clock went off at my new usual time, which Uncle Jake calls "zero-dark-thirty." Of course, Uncle Jake wasn't in the room. He was already out somewhere doing some kind of exercise. I've begun to think that maybe Uncle Jake doesn't sleep at all. I never see him go to bed at night; I never see him get up in the morning. His bed is always made. So I wasn't surprised that he wasn't in the room. But what happened next did surprise me.

"Get up!" Uncle Jake shouted as he burst into the room.

"I am up!" I told him.

"Come on, then! I got you a present."

"A present?" I already knew not to expect anything normal. In fact, I pretty much expected something *painful*.

"Yeah . . . a little something for you. Come on!"

I put on my shorts, shirt, and running shoes, and followed Uncle Jake downstairs.

"It's in the garage . . . ," said Uncle Jake as we headed out the door and through the backyard toward the garage. I wondered what in the world he could have in there. A new bike maybe? A go-kart? No, I knew this would be something more, should I say, "practical."

He opened the door to the garage and I walked in. I looked around. Nothing.

"What?" I asked him.

"What?" he replied.

"What is it?" I asked, still not seeing anything new in the garage.

"Look up," said Uncle Jake with a big smile on his face.

Slowly, I began to look up, with no idea what to expect. Then I saw it, staring back at me. A pull-up bar.

"What do you think?" Uncle Jake asked me.

It was a crazy-looking—and kind of scary—thick metal bar bolted onto two heavy-duty pieces of wood.

"I made it last night, while you were sleeping."

I guess I should have been happy. Or thankful. But I was SCARED and NERVOUS and EMBARRASSED because I already knew that I couldn't do a single pull-up! And now here I was with Uncle Jake about to see exactly how weak I really was!!

As I stood there thinking all these horrible thoughts, Uncle Jake jumped up and did twenty-five pull-ups—like it was nothing. "This is a good bar," he told me. "Give it a try. Here." He had built a little box for me to step on so I could reach the pull-up bar. He pushed the box under the bar and said, "Step on up, and let's see what you've got."

It seemed like a YEAR PASSED as I stepped up onto

the box and slowly reached toward the pull-up bar.
I grabbed ahold of it. It was much thicker than the
pull-up bar at school, which made it even harder to
hold on to. And then, just like the last day of school, I
pulled as hard as I could . . . but nothing happened.
I tried again and even grunted a little to try to prove
to Uncle Jake that I was *really* trying. But the grunting
didn't do much. Uncle Jake stood there and watched.
After a few more seconds, I lost my grip and slipped
off the bar.

   "Sorry, Uncle Jake," I told him, embarrassed at my
strength—or should I say COMPLETE LACK OF STRENGTH.
   "Don't be sorry," he replied. "Sorry won't get you
stronger. Now here is what we are going to do. . . ." He

took another box he had made, which was taller than the first one, and put it under the bar. "Step up on this box, grab the bar, and then jump up until your chin is over the bar. Then I want you to hold yourself up there as long as you can, and when you can't hold it any longer, come down as slowly as you possibly can."

I followed his instructions. I grabbed the bar, jumped up, and got my chin over the bar. I held myself up for a few seconds, and then, when I couldn't stay up any longer, I came down as slowly as I could.

As soon as I got to the bottom and my feet touched the box, Uncle Jake sounded off, "Now do it again!" I did. The next time, my muscles were already tired, so I couldn't hold myself up as long, and I came down faster. "Again!" Uncle Jake yelled again. I did it again. And again. And again. Finally, when I could barely get myself up over the bar and basically dropped right down again, Uncle Jake said, "Okay. Now take a break. When I joined the Navy, I could barely do seven pull-ups. But the Navy gave me a program, and I stuck with it—I still do it today. Now I can do about fifty of them pretty easily. You wanna know how you get good at doing pull-ups?"

"How?"

"By doing pull-ups! And by the time the summer is over, you will be doing *at least* ten pull-ups. Ten pull-ups, in a row, by the time you go back to school. How do you think that sounds?"

I was thrilled. I was going to be able to do ten pull-ups! I wouldn't be the laughingstock of gym class anymore! "I think that sounds AWESOME!" I told him.

"Well, remember, those pull-ups aren't going to happen by themselves. You are going to have to *earn* them, with hard work and dedication—understand?"

"I understand." And I did understand—this was going to be hard work—but it was going to be worth it.

"All right, next set!" Uncle Jake barked. I stepped back up on the box, grabbed the pull-up bar, jumped up, and started all over again, on my path to ten straight pull-ups.

CHAPTER 9: THE EIGHTS

I learned a lot today. The first thing I learned was about "knowledge." See, so far, most of what Uncle Jake has taught me about being a warrior has been exactly what you think being a warrior is. Like being strong and knowing how to fight. Everyone knows a warrior has to do those things. DUH!

But what a lot of people don't know, and I know I sure didn't, was that a warrior has to be SMART. Uncle Jake told me about all the things you have to know when you are a soldier. Things like this:

1. One gallon of water weighs 8.35 pounds, and the average person needs at least one half gallon a day to survive. Soldiers have to know that so they know how much water to take on missions. COOL!

Aren't you afraid of water?

2. Warriors must know how to read a map so they know where they are and how to get where they are going. Did you know in the military they don't use feet or yards or miles to measure things? Instead they use something called a "click," which stands for "kilometer." It is a little bit shorter than a mile and is made up of 1,000 meters, which are a little bit longer than a yard.

3. Warriors need to know A LOT of stuff about electronics. Like how to work satellite radios. Did you know the satellites that a radio uses to talk are in "geosynchronous" orbit around the earth? That means they are 22,000 nautical miles (which is like a regular mile, but a little bit longer) above the earth, and they stay at that same spot above the earth the whole time. WOW! That even sounds smart!

4. Warriors have to know history so they can learn what worked in past battles and what didn't. Did you know that it is always better to be on higher ground than your enemy? TRUE!

5. Warriors have to learn other languages so they can talk to people in other countries

they travel to. Did you know *hujambo* means "hello" in Swahili—the language they speak in Kenya and some other parts of Africa? Wicked cool!

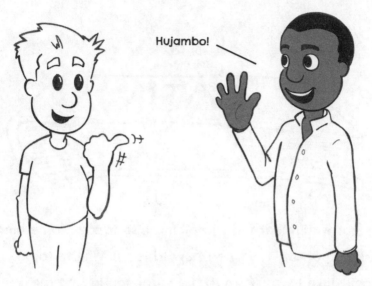

Hujambo!

6. Finally, and most important, a warrior's best weapon is the mind. They have to use their minds to figure out how to beat the enemy: How to catch them off guard. How to attack where the enemy is weak. How to OUTSMART the enemy. You can't do that if you aren't SMART!

Warriors have to be smart, which means they have to learn a lot. UH-OH! I know what you are thinking! I already told you that I'm not smart. Like I said, I had a HORRIBLE year in school. I don't even know my times tables yet!

But wait! I learned something else today—something very important: I learned how to learn. When I told Uncle Jake I wasn't smart, he laughed. He told me he didn't do well in school, either, when he was a kid. School just didn't seem important to him then. But when he got in the Navy, he realized he HAD TO LEARN a bunch of stuff. Luckily, one of his boot camp instructors taught him how to learn.

Uncle Jake asked me which number was the hardest to learn the times table for. For me it was the eights. There is no pattern or anything to them. They are just crazy. Crazy eights.

Uncle Jake went to my mom's desk and brought back some three-by-five index cards. He told me I was going to make flash cards. I told him I already had flash cards that they gave me in school. He said that those didn't work. I had to MAKE them.

So I started, writing the problem on one side and the answer on the other. 1 × 8 = 8. 2 × 8 = 16. 3 × 8 = 24. 4 × 8 = 32. 5 × 8 = 40, all the way up to 13 × 8. I told him we didn't have to know 8 × 13. He told me he didn't care! I didn't even know what 8 × 13 was AT ALL. He told me to figure it out. So I added thirteen eights until I got 104. Then he made me make the flash cards over again, but with the 8 first. 8 × 1 = 8. 8 × 2 = 16. All the way to 8 × 13 = 104. And when I got to 8 × 13, I remembered it was 104. Wait! I think I LEARNED it.

When I was done, Uncle Jake picked up the pile, shuffled the cards, and started holding them up in front of me, testing me one at a time. If it was an easy one that I got right, he would put it on the bottom of the deck. If it was a hard one that I didn't know, he made me figure it out by adding eights and then put that card only a few cards deeper in the pile so I would see it again soon. The next time I saw that card, like 8 × 7, I would remember a little better that it was 56. He would then put it a little deeper in the deck.

Eventually, when I REALLY KNEW the card and answered it as soon as I saw it, he would put it in a separate pile on the desk. That meant I knew it.

After about fifteen minutes, every card was in the "I knew it" pile.

Then Uncle Jake picked it up and went through the whole deck again. I only missed 8 × 6 and 8 × 12. He put them back into the deck and the next time I remembered them. 8 × 6 = 48 and 8 × 12 = 96. Every other card was in the "I knew it" pile.

He then picked up the "I knew it" pile and went through it again. I GOT THEM ALL RIGHT. EVERY SINGLE ONE.

"See!" Uncle Jake said. "You're not DUMB. You just need to APPLY yourself."

"What does that mean?" I asked him.

"It means work hard. Focus. Give one hundred percent. You see, no one is BORN knowing the times tables—or anything else! You have to LEARN and you have to learn EVERYTHING. That means you have to actually study and work until you know. Of course, this will be easier for some people than others."

He then explained to me that every person has stuff that they are good at and stuff they are not. Some kids can learn more easily. Some kids can run faster. Some kids can do more pull-ups. Some people are even naturally good at everything. He also told me that I was naturally good at drawing. He has seen some of my artwork from school and other drawings I made around the house. He asked me if I practiced a lot to get good at art, and when I told him no, he said I was a natural. Then he told me that just about anybody

can be good at just about anything—if they work hard.

He was right. Here I was, ten years old, and I had never actually focused on learning the times tables. I just thought I should know them like my friend Joshua. He seemed to know them as soon as he saw them. I thought I should be the same way. But that isn't the way it works. You have to apply yourself and work hard to learn things.

And that's the last thing I learned today. I'm not dumb. I'm actually pretty smart. I learned the eights 100 percent in about twenty minutes. I just need to work hard.

CHAPTER 10: JIU-JITSU

Today Uncle Jake took me to my first jiu-jitsu class. It was at a place called Victory MMA. If you don't know what MMA is, it's mixed martial arts. And if you don't know what that is, it's when the people on TV go into a cage and fight each other. I couldn't believe what I was getting into! I figured I was a DEAD MAN.

When we walked into Victory MMA, it looked pretty cool but also PRETTY SCARY! There were punching bags hanging everywhere and two boxing rings and a real fighting cage like the ones on TV.

And then upstairs a bunch of mats on the ground. In fact, the whole floor was a giant mat. Even the walls had mats on them! Awesome! There were about fifteen kids in the jiu-jitsu class Uncle Jake had picked out for me. They didn't look too tough. They were all different sizes, some bigger than me, some smaller than me. The instructor didn't look like I thought he would. He wasn't a big superhero-looking guy. In fact, he was not very tall and just looked like a normal man. He called me out on the mat.

"Get out here, kid!" he said in the kind of voice that makes you think you better listen.

Uncle Jake was doing some paperwork, so I figured I might as well get out there. I took one step onto the mat and—"STOP!" he yelled at me. "Take off your shoes, kid! No shoes on the mat!"

I sat down on the bench and took off my shoes. I walked out on the mat. "Everyone line up!" the instructor said in a stern voice.

"Takedown time. Winner stays, losers out. Two pairs, get started."

Two pairs of kids walked out onto the mat. The rest of us stayed lined up on the wall. The coach shouted, "Go!" and the two pairs of kids slapped hands and then started fighting. But they weren't punching each other. They were gripping each other's arms, grabbing wrists, pushing heads, and then, suddenly, one would shoot in, grab the other kid's legs, and slam him to the mat. I figured out quickly that was a "takedown." Whoever got taken down had to go to the end of the line. The kid that took the other kid down got to stay in and go against the next kid in line.

Soon it was my turn, and I was pretty nervous. But I was going against a kid that was smaller than me. I thought I could definitely take him down. I walked over and held out my hand to the other kid. We shook hands. He said his name was Thor. I said, "Really?" He said yes. "That's your real name?" I asked him again. He said yes, again. His actual name was THOR! I told him my name was Marc. Now that we were face-to-face, he was even smaller than I thought and definitely smaller than THOR from the comic book. He asked if I was ready. I said yes, and then we slapped hands and started to fight. Before I knew it, he put his hand in my face, which kind of startled me and made me blink. In the split second that my eyes were closed from the blink, Thor was underneath me, grabbing my legs and launching me into the air. It took him about one second to slam me into the mat. And he was smaller than me!

I got to the end of the line. The next kid I went with was bigger than me. We slapped hands, and this time I kept my hands up by my head to keep him away from my face. He grabbed my wrist and started to pull it down toward the ground. When I tried to pull it back up, he let go and dove at my legs. BOOM! I was on the ground again!

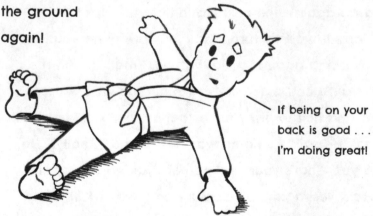

If being on your back is good . . . I'm doing great!

The next round, Uncle Jake was watching. I got slammed again. And again. And again. By big kids and little kids and kids the same size as me. And even though it was tough and I didn't like losing, it was also

AWESOME. These kids knew how to fight. They knew how to win. Even King Kenny would get slammed by these kids. And it's not because they are big or strong or fast. It's because they *know something*. They had learned this skill and they can use it. And it is something I can learn, too.

The next thing we did was called grappling. That meant that once we were on the ground from the takedown, we had to try to fight on the ground. Not with punches or kicks, but with wrestling moves and something called "jiu-jitsu." But this wasn't like other martial arts I have seen where people are standing in line kicking air. This was like real fighting.

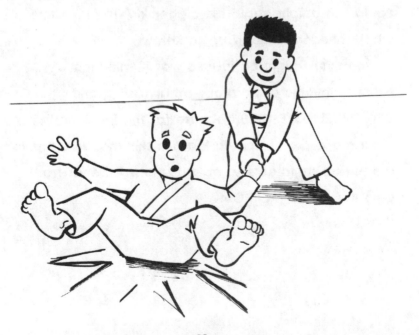

And the first thing that I learned was that I DIDN'T KNOW ANYTHING ABOUT FIGHTING. Once you hit the ground in jiu-jitsu, the other guy is trying to make you "tap out," which means give up. They would grab my arm or my wrist or my shoulder and move it to a place where it wasn't supposed to go. It would hurt just a little bit, then I would tap out, and they would let me go.

I couldn't believe how good they were. I couldn't believe how even the littler kids could easily make me TAP OUT!

And once again, it was just because they had knowledge. They had learned jiu-jitsu and now they could win a fight against a bigger kid. This is exactly what I needed to stand up to Kenny!

So my first night of jiu-jitsu was humiliating, exhausting, kind of painful, embarrassing, and COMPLETELY AWESOME because for the first time in my life, I realized that I could learn a skill that would give me the ability to defend myself and my friends from guys like Kenny. FREEDOM!

CHAPTER 11: HYDROPHOBIA

I THOUGHT I WAS GOING TO DIE TODAY. Or more specifically, DROWN! Uncle Jake knows that I DON'T LIKE WATER. AT ALL. But he says I have to learn how to swim. He told me that two-thirds of the earth is covered in water. I told him my neighborhood was ALL LAND. But he is right. I was embarrassed last year at Mount Tom when I couldn't play any games or enjoy the field trip AT ALL. Instead, I sat on the beach, which was okay for a little while in the morning. But by lunchtime, it was SWELTERING. And I was sweating. All the other kids jumped in the water and cooled off and played Chicken, and Sharks and Minnows, and Marco Polo. And what did I do? Sat in the sun sweating and getting sunburned. YUCK!

But the problem is that no matter how hot I was, I was even more worried about getting in the water. I had never learned how to swim! Once, when I was about four, I fell into something called a koi pond. If you don't know what one of those is, it's a little fake pond with goldfish in it. People put them in their yards. They aren't that big, but when you're four, they're big enough. Anyway, I was standing there looking at the fish in the little koi pond, and I decided to take a step into the water. What I didn't know was that koi ponds are kind of like giant plastic cereal bowls buried in the ground—slippery plastic. As soon as I stepped in, I slipped on the plastic and fell completely underwater.

My mom says that I got pulled out right away, but it sure didn't feel like it. I felt like I was down there, underwater, and COMPLETELY HELPLESS, forever. I never wanted to feel like that again, so ever since that day, I have avoided the water. Because I'M SCARED of it. There, I said it. I'm scared of the water. Uncle Jake says it's called hydrophobia—the fear of water. Well, whatever you call it, I got it.

That is what made today so cool. Uncle Jake took me down to a place called Bird Bridge. It is a bridge that goes over a slow-moving river. When it gets hot out, a lot of the older kids go down there and hang around and jump off and swim. It is out in the woods, and it has a little beach on one side of the river and a bank on the other side. I was excited when we headed down there. During the car ride, I didn't feel scared of the water at all. Maybe it was because Uncle Jake was with me, or because he had told me I had to learn to swim, and I accepted that fact. But I wasn't scared at all while I was in the car.

UNTIL WE GOT TO THE RIVER. As soon as the car stopped, my heart started POUNDING. I looked at the river. The water was dark. It looked black—LIKE THE KOI POND WHERE I ALMOST DIED, BUT BIGGER!

Uncle Jake could tell I was scared. After telling me to calm down, he said that I didn't have to go in if I didn't want to, which made me feel like a complete wimp. So now I was feeling terrified and wimpy!

Uncle Jake pulled off his shirt and jumped in the water. He swam across to the other side and back. Then he disappeared underwater. He was gone. I waited. And waited. Then I started to get nervous. Then I started to panic! I knew he must be drowning, caught by a vine or a fish or a monster or something, but I KNEW he was underwater, DROWNING!

Then he popped up laughing and got out of the water. He asked me to come on down to the water's edge and wade in. I asked him if he was going to push me in, and he promised he wouldn't. He told me that people are usually scared of things that they don't understand. I needed to understand that water wasn't going to hurt me as long as I respected it and learned to handle myself in it. So I walked down and put my feet in. Uncle Jake encouraged me to go a little bit deeper. Then a little deeper.

As I waded into the water, Uncle Jake pointed up to the bridge. "By the end of the summer, you're going to jump off that bridge and swim back and forth across this river."

"I don't know, Uncle Jake," I told him. "That bridge is tall, and in case you forgot, I don't even know how to swim!"

Uncle Jake got out of the water, climbed to the top of the bridge, screamed, "HOO-YAH!" and jumped in.

HOO-YAH!

"That looked like fun, right?" he said when he surfaced. I had to admit that it did.

"By the end of the summer, that will be you."

By this time, I was standing comfortably in the water up to my knees. This wasn't too bad.

Then Uncle Jake said, "Okay, time for your head to go under."

WHAT??!! My toes, my feet—that's fine. MY HEAD? NO WAY!

Uncle Jake could see that I froze up and I did not want to do it. He calmed me down and convinced me to stay in the water. He stood there and dunked his head a bunch of times, laughing and howling every time he pulled his head out. I have to admit that it looked kind of fun. Then he started yelling. But not at me—he was yelling at the woods, at the river, at the world. And not in a bad way, but like he was having the time of his life.

"AAHHWOOOOOOOOO!" he was howling, every time his head came out of the water. "AAAHHWOOOOOOO!"

He said that in the SEAL Teams they yelled "HOO-YAH" when they had to do something they didn't want to do or something they were scared to do. He said yelling loud relieved the tension of being scared. He told me to give a yell and see how it felt.

"AAAHHHHWOOOOO!" I yelled. Then again. "AAAAAAAHHHHWOOOOOOOO!"

"Louder!" he told me.

"AAAAAAHHHHWOOOOOOO!!" I yelled again and again. It felt good to let out all the fear. I did it over and over again, with Uncle Jake matching my yells, louder and louder. Then, suddenly, Uncle Jake yelled out, "Now dunk your head! AAAHHHWOOOOOO!"

Without thinking, I dunked my head completely under the water and whipped it out yelling, "AAAAAHWOOOOOOOOOOOOOOOO!!!!" I did it. It was fun, so I did it again! Then again!

Then, for a few more minutes, Uncle Jake and I sat out there dunking our heads and yelling at the top of our lungs and laughing. Finally, the rush settled down, and we walked out of the water.

"That's good for today," Uncle Jake told me.

"Yes, yes it is," I said back.

We walked back to the car, dried off, and got in.

As we drove away, I realized something: I wasn't ready to swim yet. But I was not scared anymore.

CHAPTER 12: DISCIPLINE EQUALS FREEDOM

BEEP! BEEP! BEEP! BEEP! BEEP! BEEP! BEEP! BEEP!

My morning alarm clock blasted in my ears. I listened to it for a few seconds. Then I reached over and hit the snooze button. That felt sooooooo good. I just didn't feel like getting up. I wanted to sleeeeeeep. . . . I closed my eyes and comfortably faded back into a deep sleep. . . .

In the distance, I heard the door open. Just as it registered in my groggy brain that it had to be Uncle Jake, I heard him say, "Marc?" Before I could answer him, the noise hit me like a freight train: *CLANG! CLANG! CLANG! CLANG!* It was the garbage can and the broomstick again.

"Okay. Okay. I'll get up," I told Uncle Jake. I must not have sounded very enthusiastic, because Uncle Jake called me out.

"What's wrong with you, Marc? Why weren't you down in the garage this morning for your workout?"

"Well . . ." I didn't know what to say.

"'Well' what?" Uncle Jake asked me.

"Well, I don't know," I told him. "I just . . . I'm just . . . I'm tired."

"Tired? What does tired have to do with anything?"

"Well. You know. I'm tired. I worked out all last week. I did jiu-jitsu classes. Plus, we went to the river. With so much stuff going on, I'm just tired. I think I need some rest."

"If you need rest, you go to sleep earlier. You don't sleep in, and you don't miss workouts. Even if you can't perform at a high level, showing up and doing something is still a thousand times better than not showing up at all."

"Well, it's not just that," I admitted. "This program is taking up all my time. I'm getting tired of doing so much. Maybe I could just get the chance to relax and watch some TV sometime. I could use a little freedom to do what I want."

Come back to me, buddy!

My argument seemed to make sense in my head. Shouldn't I relax a little bit? A little TV can't be that bad, right? I just wanted a little freedom.

Uncle Jake sat and looked at me. He wasn't mad. But his face looked like he almost felt sorry for me. Like I didn't know anything about anything.

"We all want freedom, Marc. All of us. That is what I want in my life. That is what my friends and I fought for overseas. Freedom is the best thing in the world. But freedom isn't free. If you want true freedom in life, you have to have discipline. Do you know what discipline is, Marc?"

I wasn't 100 percent sure, but I thought I had an idea. "Doesn't discipline mean you follow the rules?" I said.

"That's one kind of discipline," Uncle Jake said, "but it isn't as simple as just following the rules people give you. The most important part of discipline is following rules that you set for yourself. It is doing things you might not always feel like doing—things that make you better." Then Uncle Jake started getting really intense. "Listen, if you want freedom from being bullied at school by Kenny, you have to have the discipline to go to jiu-jitsu class and learn the skills to defeat him. If you want freedom from ridicule when you do pull-ups at school, you have to have the discipline to train so that you can do pull-ups.

"If you want the freedom to swim in the water and enjoy your school trip, you need the discipline to overcome your fear of the water and learn how to swim. What about school? Do you want to be free of being stumped on tests and not knowing the answer to questions in class? Then you need the discipline to study and learn the material they teach you. When you get older, you are going to want financial freedom—that means having enough money to do what you want without worrying about it. The only way you are going to get financial freedom is by having financial discipline—by saving money and not wasting it on things you don't need. And all that discipline starts with getting up early in the morning."

"Well, I'm up now," I told Uncle Jake.

"I know you are," he replied. "But you are only up because I woke you up. I made you get up. That's called 'imposed discipline'—when someone else makes you do what they want you to do. What you need is called SELF-DISCIPLINE. That is when *you* take control of yourself. When you push yourself. When you make yourself do the hard things. That is what gives you freedom. Does that make sense to you?"

"I think it does," I told Uncle Jake.

"You need to do better than think it does. You need

to understand. Explain to me what you think self-discipline means."

I was nervous because I wasn't 100 percent sure I understood. But it did make sense to me, so I figured I would give it a try. And it's not like I had much of a choice anyway, with Uncle Jake staring at me, waiting for an answer.

"I think it means this, Uncle Jake," I told him. "We all want freedom in life. We want to be able to do what we want. We want to live free. But in order to get freedom, we have to work for it. Work hard. We have to earn that freedom. Freedom requires discipline. So even though sometimes discipline seems like it is trapping you and making you do things that you don't want to do, discipline is the thing that will set you free. Discipline equals freedom."

DISCIPLINE EQUALS FREEDOM

"That's right, Marc. Perfect. Discipline equals freedom. So let's get up and get to work!"

"Is that what keeps you motivated, Uncle Jake?" I asked, wondering how he stays so fired up all the time.

"Motivated?" Uncle Jake replied. "I don't worry about motivation, because motivation comes and goes. It's just a feeling. You might feel motivated to do something, and you might not. The thing that keeps you on course and keeps you on the warrior path isn't motivation. It is discipline. Discipline gets you out of bed. Discipline gets you onto the pull-up bar. Discipline gets you to grind it out in jiu-jitsu class. If you do those things only when you are motivated to do them, you might do them only fifty percent of the time. Sure, it's nice when motivation is there, but you can't count on motivation. You have to rely on the personal discipline you develop. Like you said: Discipline equals freedom. Got it?"

"Yes, Uncle Jake, I do."

"Good. Then let's go down to the garage and get busy."

And we did just that!

CHAPTER 13: PULL-UP NUMBER ONE

YES!!!!!!!!!

I DID IT! Finally, after eighteen days of training, TODAY I DID MY FIRST PULL-UP. BY MYSELF!!!

It was pretty easy, too. I did some push-ups at the beginning of the workout, and I actually got my record there, too, with twenty-two. Then I did some sit-ups and a few squats.

Then it was time to do pull-ups.

So I went and got the big box that Uncle Jake built for me to jump off of when I do pull-ups. But when I slid it underneath the pull-up bar, Uncle Jake said, "No."

I was puzzled. "Why? You don't want me to do pull-ups today?"

"Quite the opposite, Marc," he answered. "You are ready to do an *actual* pull-up today."

Oh no! I thought to myself. For the previous three weeks, all of my "pull-up" workouts haven't included any actual pull-ups. I have only been doing something called "negatives," where I jump up off the big box so I can get my chin over the bar. Once I got up there, I would try to hold it as long as I could. Then I would slowly come down, lowering myself as slowly as possible, fighting it the whole way down. Once I was at the bottom, I would jump up and get my chin over the bar again. So although this was a "pull-up workout," I wasn't actually doing any pull-ups.

"I don't think I'm quite ready yet," I told Uncle Jake.

Y'know, I'm thinking maybe I'll leave the real pull-ups to the pull-up professionals. . . .

"Oh, you're ready. And even if you aren't, you need to try. We have to assess your progress."

"Well, I am definitely holding myself up there for a longer time now," I told him. "When I started, I was only able to hold myself up for a couple of seconds. Now I can hold myself up for over thirty seconds."

"Well, that's good progress," Uncle Jake said, "but your goal isn't holding yourself up. Your goal is to do an actual pull-up. So let's see what you've got."

Uncle Jake pulled away the tall box that allowed me to jump my chin up over the bar and replaced it with the short box that made it so I could barely even reach the bar.

"There you go," he said. "Giddyup."

I was filled with fear. Every time I had tried in the past, no matter how hard I pulled, I could never get my chin over the bar. Now, with Uncle Jake standing right here, after all the work he has done with me, I just didn't think I would be able to do it. I stood there looking at the bar.

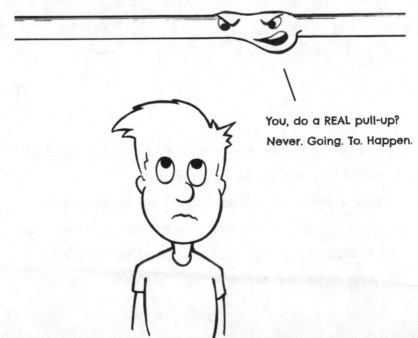

You, do a REAL pull-up?
Never. Going. To. Happen.

"Well? What are you waiting for?"

I slowly stepped up on the box and reached up for the bar. The bar was cool in my hands, and I noticed something that I hadn't thought about: my grip. In the past, my grip always felt like it was going to slip off the bar. My grip felt different now. It felt strong.

I concentrated, and then, after taking a big breath, I pulled. And I went up. And up!

And up! And soon my chin cleared the top of the bar! YES! I HAD DONE IT!

I let myself down slowly and dropped off the bar. I looked at my uncle. He had a big smile on his face.

A BIG smile! He was happy! And I was even happier. It felt so good.

I looked at Uncle Jake and yelled, "YEAH!!!!" as I curled both of my fists toward my shoulders like I had seen weight lifters do in magazines. And I could actually tell that, for the first time in my life, I was starting to get some muscles. Nothing huge, but they were certainly there. "MUSCLEMAN MARC!" I shouted, as proud as I could be.

Then I saw Uncle Jake's smile disappear.

"Hold on there, Muscleman," said Uncle Jake. I didn't know what was wrong, but something was.

"I think it's a bit early for a celebration."

"Early? I just did the first pull-up of my life! I think it is the perfect time for a celebration!" I told Uncle Jake.

"That's a problem."

"A problem? Why is a pull-up a problem?"

"Not the pull-up, Marc. The celebration. It is way too early for you to be celebrating."

"But I just did my first pull-up. EVER!"

"But your goal isn't one pull-up. It is ten pull-ups. You did one. Sure, you have a reason to be happy— one pull-up is better than zero. But it is a long way from ten. No matter what you are doing in life, you can't take your eyes off the long-term goal—

especially to celebrate. You can assess. You can try to figure out some lessons learned from what you did right and what you did wrong. You can even do a little celebrating for the small victories. But don't go overboard. You need to keep your head in the game. So come over here, give me a high five, and then get back over there and start doing more work on the pull-up bar. This is only the beginning."

I walked over to Uncle Jake, who brought his hand up in the air.

I slapped it hard, and he said, "Solid work. Now get back over there and get after it."

"Yes, sir," I told him.

I walked back over to the bar and actually did

three more individual pull-ups before I needed to get the bigger box to jump up with. Then I did a bunch of the negative work, coming down as slow as I could. Knowing that I had already made some real progress made me focus even more. Ten pull-ups is a long way away. But I started to think I might just get there.

CHAPTER 14: FLASH CARD FURY

I am starting to learn some things about Uncle Jake
that are very important to understand. While yesterday
I learned not to celebrate too early, today I realized
something else: Good is never good enough! Today
was a perfect example.

I was sitting down in the afternoon while Uncle Jake
was at the store. I decided to watch some TV, which
is something I haven't exactly had a lot of time to do
lately! When Uncle Jake got home and saw me sitting
there watching TV, he didn't look very happy with me.
At all.

"What are you doing, Marc?" he asked with a
disappointed tone.

"Just sitting here watching some TV."

"I can see that. Why? Don't you have anything better to do?"

"Well, we already worked out today. And my room is clean. And I did the dishes and cleaned the kitchen. So I'm pretty much all caught up with everything."

"Really? What about your times tables?"

"My times tables?" I had been hoping he would ask that! I had been studying hard and knew all the tables from one to thirteen by heart at this point. "I know all of them. Every flash card. One hundred percent."

"One hundred percent? Good. Go get them."

"The flash cards?"

"Yes, the flash cards. I will be the judge."

"Okay." I ran up to my room to get my flash cards. When I came back down, Uncle Jake was pulling something out of his gym bag. It looked like a big watch.

"What's that?" I asked him.

"A stopwatch."

"A what?"

"A stopwatch. To time you."

"Time me?"

"Yes. Time you. To see if you are fast enough."

"Fast enough? This isn't a race!" I complained.

"Everything is a race," replied Uncle Jake with an evil smile on his face. "Give me the cards."

Hesitating and a little nervous, I handed the cards to Uncle Jake. We sat down at the table.

"Ready?" Uncle Jake asked.

"Ready," I replied, starting to feel the pressure.

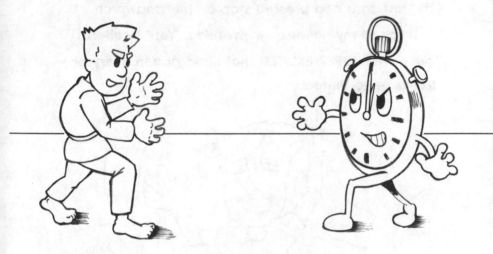

"GO!!!!" He pressed the start button on the stopwatch and held up the first card. It was 5 × 3.

"Fifteen!" I said. He held up the next card, which read: 2 × 4.

"Eight," I barked.

He held up the next card. He held up 9 × 6, which for some reason, maybe the pressure or the stopwatch, I blanked on for a few seconds. Then I dug through my brain and remembered. "Fifty-four!" I yelled.

"Slow," Uncle Jake said as he held up the next card.

We went through the whole pile. There were some that I hesitated on, and I actually missed two, but since I corrected them before he could even put them back in the pile, that meant I didn't have to answer them again. As soon as I finished, Uncle Jake slapped down the last card and pressed stop on the stopwatch.

I raised my hands over my head. "Yes!" I called out—I was SUPER EXCITED that I had gotten every one of the cards right.

"'Yes' what?" Uncle Jake asked me. Now I knew from the first pull-up I did that I should never celebrate too early. But this wasn't early. The mission was accomplished—or so I thought.

"Well, Uncle Jake, I'm excited because I made it through all the times tables. That means I learned. Thanks so much for helping me, Uncle Jake. I couldn't have done it without your help."

"That's not true. I only helped you learn one group of numbers; you learned the rest on your own. Once you learned how to learn, you learned on your own."

"I guess that's kinda true," I said, not sure where Uncle Jake was heading with this conversation.

"But you aren't done yet."

"I'm not?"

"No. It took you six minutes and thirty-seven seconds to get through the flash cards. You should be doing it in less than four minutes."

"Four minutes? Really?"

"Really," Uncle Jake replied. "I want you to know these answers so well that there isn't any hesitation whatsoever. None. Understand?"

"Yes. I understand."

Uncle Jake continued, "And that is the way you should do everything—the absolute best you can. Give it everything you've got. One hundred percent. That will get you where you want to be."

And with that, I started studying again, now timing

myself using Uncle Jake's stopwatch. I was GOING TO
GET THERE!

CHAPTER 15: TAP OUT!

Today was crazy, unbelievable, nuts, and AMAZING at jiu-jitsu class!

I got to class, and we did the normal warm-up stuff that we always do: run around the mat, push-ups, some sit-ups, some rolls, and all that basic stuff. Then we did our drills where we worked on our basic moves: arm locks and sweeps and the "escaping the mount" position. We were about halfway done with class when a new kid showed up. It was his first day. He had never done jiu-jitsu before.

While we were drilling some moves, I saw the instructor going over the basics with this kid and showing him what jiu-jitsu was all about, what the basic positions were, and, also, most important, how to tap out.

Then it was time to *roll*. Rolling in jiu-jitsu is when you are sparring against your opponent. It is kind of like a real fight, except without kicking or punching. But you learn pretty quick that on-the-ground kicking and punching aren't as important as people think. What is more important is being in the right position so you can control your opponent and then, when the time is right, make him tap out with some kind of joint lock or choke. A joint lock is when you trap your opponent's arm or leg in such a way that they can't move it and then you actually move it in the opposite direction—the direction an arm or a leg is not supposed to go!

My jiu-jitsu instructor

Jiu-jitsu is fun and safe. I make sure everyone follows the rules, trains safely, and has a great time!

But don't worry, you don't hurt your opponents. As soon as they feel the tension on their arm or leg, all they have to do is tap out and you let go. It is all over. It is the same thing with a choke. You put your arms in a position around their neck to choke them, and in a second, they tap out. We also learned to ONLY DO JIU-JITSU IN JIU-JITSU CLASS WITH THE INSTRUCTOR THERE. It is important to have an instructor around when we train to make sure we are practicing safe and effective jiu-jitsu.

I rolled with a couple of the other kids in class for the first two rounds. Then the instructor called to me, "Come on over here, Marc."

I went right over to the instructor and said, "Yes, sir?"

"Marc, this is Jaden. Jaden, this is Marc."

I shook hands with the new kid. "Hi Jaden."

"I want you to roll with Jaden, please, Marc."

"Yes, sir."

Then the instructor looked at Jaden and said, "Just relax and have fun. And remember, if it hurts or if it is uncomfortable, just tap and Marc will let you go and you can start again. It's okay to tap. It just means you are learning. Okay?"

"Okay," Jaden said.

We walked over to an open area of the mat. Jaden was a little bit smaller than me, but not too much. Just maybe an inch or two shorter. I held out my hand, and we shook hands.

As soon as we stepped back from shaking hands, Jaden rushed at me!! I guess he wasn't going to relax like the instructor asked him to!!! As he moved forward, he tried to get ahold of my hands and arms, grabbing at them like a giant crab.

I pushed his hands away, and as he came forward, I ducked underneath his arms and easily grabbed ahold of his legs. Then I drove forward like I had been taught, a classic double-leg takedown!

When we got on the ground, Jaden really started going crazy. He was pushing and bucking and squirming around—but he didn't know what he was doing. He didn't know what to push or when to buck or where to squirm. I easily got the position of full mount on him, where I was sitting on his belly like I was riding a horse.

When I got there, Jaden pushed his hands into my chest to try to get me off him. This was something that people who don't know jiu-jitsu usually do: they try to push you off them—and I knew just what to do when that happens. In an instant, I spun to the side and threw one leg over his head.

I held on to one of his arms with my arms, squeezed my knees together, and leaned back. As I went back, I felt Jaden squirm even more—but it was no use. I had him.

I slowly pushed my hips into his elbow joint, and very quickly, Jaden tapped out! THAT WAS IT! The first time I had ever tapped someone out! YES!

But even though I was SUPER EXCITED and FIRED UP
that I was able to tap out Jaden, I knew I needed to
stay calm and be nice to him. "Don't worry, Jaden, it
happens to everyone when they start out."

"Really?"

"Yes, really. That's what jiu-jitsu does. It is like
knowing how to play the piano or shoot a basketball—
it is just a skill that you need to practice. Once you
practice and get good at it, you will be tapping
people out, too!"

"Well, that's good. Is there anything I should have
done different?" Jaden asked.

I spent the rest of the class going over some basic
moves with Jaden. He was really happy and definitely
wanted to learn. And now that I had actually felt the
true power of jiu-jitsu, I wanted to learn more, too!

CHAPTER 16: FUELING THE MACHINE

One thing I can tell you about all this training and working out and studying is that it makes you HUNGRY! By the end of the day, I always feel like I am STARVING and ready to eat ANYTHING and EVERYTHING! And that is kind of what I have always done: just eat whatever I wanted to eat, whenever I wanted to eat it. Until tonight. Tonight I learned SOMETHING ELSE from Uncle Jake! This time about food . . .

So, like I said, when I went downstairs for dinner, I was HUNGRY and THIRSTY. My mom had made some dinner, but I was in the mood for something a little tastier. So I grabbed a bag of potato chips and poured a bunch onto my plate. Then I went into the freezer, grabbed a microwavable ham-and-cheese sandwich, and threw it in the microwave. They are TASTY! I heated it up for a couple of minutes until the cheese was oozing out of the sides. Grabbing it from the microwave, I opened the plastic bag it was in and threw it on my plate next to the pile of potato chips.

Finally, because I was thirsty, I grabbed a can of grape soda from the fridge and walked over to the table where my mom and Uncle Jake were sitting.

"How is it going?" I said as I sat down.

"Outstanding," Uncle Jake replied. "How are you doing?"

"Pretty good," I said. And right as those words came out of my mouth, Uncle Jake looked down at my plate. Then at my can of grape soda. Then back at me.

"REALLY?" he said in a stern voice, his mood changing suddenly from happy to almost angry. I had NO IDEA what he could possibly be mad at me about.

"Yeah," I mumbled under my breath. "I'm doing okay."

Uncle Jake seemed to relax a little bit and then said, "That's surprising."

"Why is that surprising, Uncle Jake?" I asked him, now truly curious as to why the heck he was acting so strange.

"It's surprising you can feel okay with all that JUNK

YOU ARE EATING!" he barked. I had no idea what he was talking about. My mom nodded in agreement.

"Junk?"

"Yes, JUNK. That is what you have on your plate right now: JUNK. It won't help your muscles to recover. It won't help you think clearly. All that junk won't help you get better."

I still didn't understand. "Wait. What? What is wrong with my food? This is what my mom buys, and this is what I eat every day."

"You eat that every day? AAAHHHGGGG!! How can you eat that every day? And it isn't the only thing that your mom buys. I got this from the same kitchen you got your food from," he said as he pointed down at his plate.

I took a look at his plate and had to admit to myself that he was right. He had a salad and some chicken on his plate. And he was drinking a big glass of milk. But I still didn't understand. "Wait, what's the difference between what you're eating and what I'm eating?"

"What's the difference? EVERYTHING. Chicken and milk have protein in them, which is used to rebuild muscles. They both also contain fat, which is needed to help your body function. And this salad has all kinds of minerals and nutrients that keep you healthy. You know how much of that good stuff is in the garbage you are eating?"

"I'm not really sure."

"NONE! ZERO! ZIP! NADA! You're eating and drinking a bunch of sugar. All that does for you is make you sick and drain your energy. You need to get a grip on your fuel intake."

"Fuel intake?" I had no idea what he meant by this. "What am I, a car?"

"You aren't a car, but a machine like a car. The food you eat is like fuel. If you put the wrong fuel in a car, the car doesn't work anymore. So you need to fix that, ASAP!"

I'm a broken-down car!!

"Okay. So what should I eat?"

"You need to eat REAL FOOD. Steak. Fish. Chicken.
Eggs. Pork. Salad. Vegetables. Nuts and seeds. Stuff that
is real food, not stuff that comes from a factory like
those potato chips . . . or that sandwich!"

"And I buy you plenty of real food, Marc. You just
need to eat it instead of the snack food," my mom
chimed in.

"Okay. Okay. I get it. Tomorrow I will start to eat real
food, like that."

"Tomorrow? What do you mean tomorrow?"

"Well, I don't want to waste this food," I told Uncle
Jake, thinking that he would at least let me enjoy this
one last tasty meal.

"Wrong answer. There is only one time to start making yourself better: NOW. You need to start now, not tomorrow, not next week, not next month, not next year. NOW. Go throw that food in the garbage and pour that soda down the drain. You need to put the right fuel in the machine."

"Yes, Uncle Jake." I looked at my mom to see if she would be upset at this waste of food, but she nodded, yes, go throw it away. I went and threw the potato chips and microwavable sandwich away and then poured the grape soda down the drain. Then I made myself a new plate with chicken and salad, and I poured myself a glass of milk.

When I sat back down, my mom said, "Just to make this easier for you, I'm not buying any more junk food. Just real food. That way you don't have the option of eating junk."

"Okay, Mom," I told her. I wasn't sure if different food would make a difference. But I did know this: If it was good enough for Uncle Jake, it was good enough for me.

CHAPTER 17: FISH IN THE WATER

I was not ready for what Uncle Jake did to me today. At least I didn't think I was.

For the past few weeks, Uncle Jake has been taking me to the river every other day. "Swim Day" he calls it. First, I waded in the water. Then, I dunked my head. Then, he taught me to tread water, which is when you just stay in one place and keep your head above water. From there, he taught me to float in the water without moving—which is called the dead-man's float! After that, he started teaching me how to swim, a basic way of swimming called the crawl stroke. It wasn't too bad. And I have been getting better and better at doing it. The last few times, I have actually been swimming without touching the bottom at all.

My new best friend . . . water!!

But when I got to the creek today, Uncle Jake said, "Today you are swimming across the creek. The whole thing. And back again."

Sure, I was feeling all good and comfortable when we drove down. But when he said those words, I nearly had a PANIC ATTACK! Swim all the way across? ARE YOU KIDDING ME?

I felt pretty good swimming along the beach side of the river. Especially because I knew if things got out of control, I could just STAND UP. But swimming across, once I got about fifteen feet from the shore, I wouldn't be able to touch the bottom. I would be helpless, just like I was back in the koi pond when I was a kid!

Alert! Water is my enemy! Abort friendship!

"I don't think I'm quite ready for that, Uncle Jake," I told him.

"You are ready. I know. And if you don't think you're ready, you better get ready, because you are doing it. Today."

"But, Uncle Jake . . ."

"No 'buts,' Marc. I'm telling you: You are ready. You are doing it."

"I'll drown!" I said. The words kind of just slipped out. I didn't really think I would drown. . . . Okay, maybe I did think that a little bit!

"You're not going to drown, Marc," Uncle Jake said, sounding pretty annoyed with me.

"I might," I told him.

"No. You're not going to drown. You are going to be perfectly fine. I won't let you drown, and I will be right next to you. In the SEAL Teams, we never do anything in the water alone, without someone watching us. No one should EVER do anything in the water alone. You need to have someone watch and make sure you are safe. It's called a 'swim buddy,' and I will be yours."

"You will?" This made me feel better. Of course Uncle Jake wouldn't let anything happen to me.

"Yes. I will. I will make sure nothing happens to you. You are ready. Now let's go."

"Okay."

We waded out into the water. I was focused. Very focused. I looked at the other side of the river, which was about thirty yards away. I figured it would take me about twenty strokes to get across.

I looked at Uncle Jake. He nodded as if to say, "Go." I guess I needed a little more than just a head nod, because I just sat there looking at him. Finally, he said, "Well?"

I said back, "'Well' what?"

He raised his voice and said, "Well . . . GO!"

I looked across the river, looked back at him again, took a deep breath, and lunged forward into the depths. Uncle Jake went right along with me, which made me feel VERY safe and very calm. I knew nothing would happen to me while Uncle Jake was right next to me. I did the stroke just the way he had taught me. IT WORKED PERFECTLY.

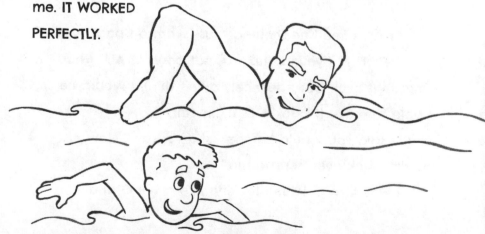

I focused on the other side, kept concentrating, and felt the comfort of having Uncle Jake right next to me. The bank on the other side got closer and closer. I started to feel for the bottom with my toes on each stroke. Finally, about five feet from the bank, my toes touched the bottom, and I pushed myself to the bank. I MADE IT! I MADE IT!

I looked over at Uncle Jake and smiled. He flashed a big smile back at me. "I MADE IT!" I yelled joyously. "I MADE IT! I MADE IT! I MADE IT! YEEEESSS! AAHHWOOOOOOOHOOOO!!!!!!"

Just as I finished my final triumphant yell, Uncle Jake disappeared underwater. I didn't know what he was doing, but he was down there for a while. When he finally came up, he was all the way on the other side of the river. I WAS ALL ALONE.

"What are you doing, Uncle Jake?" I called in a loud voice.

"You're fine!" he shouted. "Just swim on back to me."

"What??!!" I yelled. This was not cool. AT ALL. I had made it over, but I definitely didn't think I would be able to make it back! Not by myself.

"I said you would be fine—and you are. Now just swim back over here to me."

I was torn between looking like a WIMP and

possibly drowning. I decided to go with looking like a WIMP!

"Actually, Uncle Jake, I would be A LOT more comfortable if you could swim over here so you can swim back with me. PLEASE!" I hoped his understanding of how scared I was would shine through! But it didn't.

Me   Creek that eats people   Uncle Jake
who aren't Navy SEALs

"Nope. I'm not coming over. You made it there. You can make it back. Trust me."

Wait! Isn't *Trust me* something that people say when they aren't telling you the truth?? And besides, he had already told me he was going to stay close to me. How could I trust him!!! Finally, I just said, "Well, I don't think this is a very good idea. Maybe you could just please come over here and—"

Uncle Jake cut me off. "This is a VERY good idea. You know how to swim. You made it there. You can make it back. Now on the count of three, GO. One. Two. Three. GO!"

For some reason, which I may never understand, when he got to three and said, "Go," I made an instant decision. I pushed off the bank and started to swim. I felt scared and alone at first, but I just focused on the other side and kept swimming. Each stroke brought me closer and closer to Uncle Jake and the sandy little beach on the other side. Then, just when I really felt comfortable with it, I felt my foot touch the bottom. I. HAD. MADE. IT. YEESSSSSSSSS!

Uncle Jake smiled again and said, "Okay, you can hoot now. . . ."

With that, I let out the biggest

AAHHWOOOOOOO!!!!!!

I had ever yelled in my life. I looked at Uncle Jake and said, "I'm like a fish in the water!" I waited for him to yell.

"Well, Fish in the Water," he said, "just remember, you still owe me a jump off that bridge."

I sat there in silence. But the message was clear: I still have a lot to prove. And as I looked up to the top of the bridge, I knew I wasn't quite ready for that yet.

CHAPTER 18: CHASING RECORDS AND BREAKING PLATEAUS

Just when you think you know what pain is—there is more!

This week I learned about pain.

Everything had been going along smoothly, and I felt like I was doing pretty good work and making some real improvements. I was up to thirty-five push-ups, and I was doing nine repetitions of a new exercise Uncle Jake had taught me called dips. My swimming was coming along. So I was getting better and was feeling pretty strong in just about everything—except the most important thing: PULL-UPS.

That's right. Despite all the hard work I had put myself through over the last month, I was stuck on pull-ups. The most I had gotten in a row was four. And I seemed stuck there. Each workout, I would do a few more push-ups, a few more dips, a few more squats, a few more sit-ups than the last time. But for the last few workouts, I had been stuck at four pull-ups, and I didn't know what to do.

"I'm stuck, Uncle Jake. I can't get past four pull-ups. And I don't know what to do."

"Well. You've been following the workout. You've

improved what you have been eating. So. This must be a plateau."

"What's a plateau?" I asked.

"It's when you reach a level that you aren't breaking through. You're not improving the way you should be. Sometimes the body just adapts to the stress you're putting on it and stops improving."

"Oh, man," I said. "That's horrible. Does this mean I won't be able to get to ten pull-ups? Or even five?" I asked.

Uncle Jake shook his head. "No," he said, "it doesn't mean that at all. It just means we need to break through the plateau."

"How do we do that?" I wondered.

"Well, you know how I said your body has adapted to the stress put on it from working out?"

"Yeah, I guess." I was pretty sure I understood this.

"Well, here is what is happening: You make the body work hard—or you 'stress' the body—and then, in order to deal with that stress, the body builds muscle and gets stronger—or it 'adapts' to that stress."

"So my body has adapted a little?" I asked.

"Actually, your body has adapted a lot. You have gotten better in every exercise. You are just stuck. But we will get you through that."

Time to break a
couple plateaus . . .

"How?" I asked.

"Simple. More stress."

"More stress?" I didn't like the sound of that. AT ALL!

"Yes. More stress. We are going to push you harder—the hardest you've been pushed in your workouts—and we will do a workout specifically based on stressing your pull-up muscles to smash this plateau and get your pull-up numbers increasing. Be ready for a good workout tomorrow morning."

"Good? What do you mean by good?" I asked, worried that Uncle Jake's definition of the word *good* might be a little different than mine.

"I guess I mean pain. Be ready for some pain in the morning."

That's EXACTLY what I was afraid of!

This is what pain looks like.

The next morning, the workout was PSYCHO!

It started off pretty normally. We did some push-ups, then some sit-ups, then some squats. Then we got to pull-ups, and Uncle Jake said, "Today you are going to do one hundred."

"Pull-ups?" I asked in shock.

"Yes. Pull-ups. You are going to do one hundred."

"Maybe you are forgetting, but I can only do FOUR PULL-UPS, UNCLE JAKE! HOW THE HECK AM I GOING TO DO ONE HUNDRED?????" I asked.

"However you can," Uncle Jake answered. "However you can. Now get up there and get started."

I stepped up on the box, reached for the bar, and did my first set of four. "Good," Uncle Jake said. "Now do it again." I grabbed the bar and did another four. "That's eight," Uncle Jake said. "Keep going." I took a little rest, then reached up to the bar and did another three. "And that is eleven. Eighty-nine to go."

So that is what he meant. I was going to do a hundred pull-ups. But not in a row, in sets. Since I could only do four at the most, it was going to be A LOT OF SETS!

But I kept going. And going. And going. I was able to do sets of three for a while, but then around fifty, I could only do sets of two. When I got to eighty, I could only get one pull-up at a time.

Right in the middle of number eighty-seven, I felt a pain in my hand. When I got off the bar, I looked down at my right hand. One of the calluses had been ripped off. There was a trickle of blood coming out.

"I think I'm done," I said to Uncle Jake, showing him my hand.

"Thirteen more," Uncle Jake said.

"But my hand. It hurts," I told him, hoping he would have mercy on me.

"Thirteen more," Uncle Jake said again.

I stepped up onto the box and grabbed the bar. I did another one. It hurt. Then I did another one. Then I adjusted my grip a little so I was holding on with just my fingers, and I found that hurt a little less. I did another and another and then a few more.

Then, finally, I finished. ONE HUNDRED PULL-UPS.

My hands were sore and bloody. I had blood on my shirt. I was sweating. But I had done it.

"Good job, Marc," Uncle Jake said. Then, in a very serious tone, he added, "We don't quit. Ever."

I nodded. And I felt good. Really good.

The next day, Uncle Jake told me not to work out at all. And that night he took me to a movie and to the Classic Malt Shoppe for a double cheeseburger!

Three days later, I got up on the bar, and I did six pull-ups. I was on my way; the plateau had been broken—but I hadn't been.

CHAPTER 19: PRESIDENTS, CAPITALS, AND GETTYSBURG

If you thought for a minute that mastering the times tables would be enough for me to learn during the summer—think again. My uncle Jake had other ideas. He wanted me to learn a bunch of other stuff, too. Once I got the times tables in less than three minutes, he made me make flash cards for every state in America and the capital of the state. Next he wanted me to learn the name of EVERY PRESIDENT WE HAVE EVER HAD. I had no idea how I was going to do that!

So Uncle Jake sat me down. He told me to write down every single president on a piece of paper. "Like flash cards?" I asked.

"No. Not this time. Just write them down on a piece of paper. In a row or two."

"Okay." Uncle Jake walked out of the room, and I

pulled out a book from school about all the presidents. Then I wrote them all down in two rows, like he said.

Washington	Harrison
Adams	Cleveland
Jefferson	McKinley
Madison	Roosevelt
Monroe	Taft
Adams	Wilson
Jackson	Harding
Van Buren	Coolidge
Harrison	Hoover
Tyler	Roosevelt
Polk	Truman
Taylor	Eisenhower
Fillmore	Kennedy
Pierce	Johnson
Buchanan	Nixon
Lincoln	Ford
Johnson	Carter
Grant	Reagan
Hayes	Bush
Garfield	Clinton
Arthur	Bush
Cleveland	Obama
	Trump

Just as I finished up, Uncle Jake came back into my room. I showed him the list.

"Good," he said. "Now let's trailblaze."

"What's that?" I asked.

"It is another way to memorize things. Things that are longer and not direct question-and-answer. Like the presidents or the Gettysburg Address."

"What's the Gettysburg Address?" I asked.

"What's the Gettysburg Address? Really? All right, we'll get to that later. Right now, let's focus on the presidents. Look at them and memorize the first ten. I'll give you five minutes." With that, Uncle Jake walked out the door.

NOW WHAT WAS I GOING TO DO? How could I ever memorize these in five minutes????

I looked down at the paper: Washington, Adams, Jefferson, Madison, Monroe, Adams, Jackson, Van Buren, Harrison, Tyler. I read through them again: Washington, Adams, Jefferson, Madison, Monroe, Adams, Jackson, Van Buren, Harrison, Tyler. And I did it again. And again.

Then Uncle Jake came back in. "You got them memorized yet?" he asked. I thought he might be kidding. But he wasn't.

"No," I said. "Not even close."

"That's okay. No one can memorize that fast. But you can definitely memorize this easily. Now. Take one last look at those first ten. But focus on the first four."

WASHINGTON
ADAMS
JEFFERSON
MADISON

I looked down at the paper again, looking at the first four: Washington, Adams, Jefferson, Madison.

Again: Washington, Adams, Jefferson, Madison.

"Okay," Uncle Jake said as he snatched the paper away from me. "Go."

"Washington. Adams. Jefferson. Mmmmm . . . mmmmm . . ." I knew the next one began with an *M*, but I just couldn't remember the rest of it.

"Mad . . ." Uncle Jake gave me a hint.

"Madison?"

"Yes. Now. Look at the paper. And then start over again at the beginning, down the trail you already made. But try to go just a little farther down the trail each time."

I looked at the paper and saw Washington, Adams, Jefferson, Madison, MONROE.

Uncle Jake flipped the paper over. I started again. "Washington, Adams, Jefferson, Madison, and Monroe?"

"Yes," Uncle Jake said, "and who is after Monroe?"

"I actually have no idea."

"That's okay. Look at the paper again." I looked down and saw that after Monroe was ADAMS. I thought to myself: *Monroe, ADAMS, Monroe, Adams. Monroe, Adams.*

"You ready?" Uncle Jake asked.

"I guess so," I replied.

"Go. From the beginning."

"Washington, Adams, Jefferson, Madison, Monroe . . .
Adams."

"Yes!" Uncle Jake said. "That's it. Each time you
get stumped, you stop, take a look, think about how
it ties into what you know, and then go back to the
beginning of whatever you are trying to memorize—
the beginning of the trail. I just want you to finish the
first ten tonight. I will test you on them in the morning."

And that was it. It was a simple system. AND IT
WORKED! I kept repeating the presidents I knew, and
then when I got stumped, I would check the paper,
look at it and try to memorize the next one, and then
put the paper down and go back to the beginning.

I didn't always get it right. And I got stumped a few times really bad. I had to go back and look at the paper six times for Van Buren. What kind of name is Van Buren anyway? But I got them memorized.

The next morning, as soon as I rolled out of bed, Uncle Jake was there. "Go," he said.

"Go? Go where?" I asked, still a little groggy.

"The presidents! Let's hear the first ten."

"Oh yeah," I said. Those. Here we go:

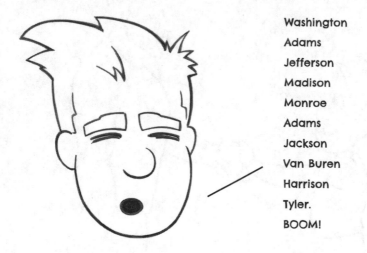

Washington
Adams
Jefferson
Madison
Monroe
Adams
Jackson
Van Buren
Harrison
Tyler.
BOOM!

Uncle Jake got a smile out of that! "Good job, Marc," he said. "Good job."

"Thanks, Uncle Jake."

We headed down for the morning workout.

"So. For the next four nights, you can keep working

on memorizing the presidents. Once you have those, you can move on to the Gettysburg Address."

"You still haven't even told me what that is, Uncle Jake."

"Well, first you have to know about the Battle of Gettysburg . . . ," Uncle Jake said. Then he told me all about it. It was a brutal battle in the Civil War near the town of Gettysburg, Pennsylvania. Almost fifty thousand men were killed or wounded in three days of fighting. After the battle was over, President Lincoln came to the site and gave a speech called the Gettysburg Address. Although the speech was only ten sentences long and President Lincoln spoke for only two minutes, my uncle Jake says it is one of the best speeches ever. I copied it out of a history book:

> Four score and seven years ago our
> fathers brought forth on this continent,
> a new nation, conceived in Liberty, and
> dedicated to the proposition that all men
> are created equal.
>
> Now we are engaged in a great civil
> war, testing whether that nation, or any
> nation so conceived and so dedicated,
> can long endure. We are met on a great

battlefield of that war. We have come to dedicate a portion of that field, as a final resting place for those who here gave their lives that that nation might live. It is altogether fitting and proper that we should do this.

But, in a larger sense, we cannot dedicate—we cannot consecrate—we cannot hallow—this ground. The brave men, living and dead, who struggled here, have consecrated it, far above our poor power to add or detract. The world will little note, nor long remember what we say here, but it can never forget what they did here. It is for us the living, rather, to be dedicated here to the unfinished work which they who fought here have thus far so nobly advanced.

It is rather for us to be here dedicated
to the great task remaining before us—
that from these honored dead we take
increased devotion to that cause for
which they gave the last full measure
of devotion—that we here highly resolve
that these dead shall not have died in
vain—that this nation, under God, shall
have a new birth of freedom—and that
government of the people, by the people,
for the people, shall not perish from the
earth.

Uncle Jake said everyone should memorize that
speech. I agree with him, and I will.

CHAPTER 20: MARC VERSUS GOLIATH ON THE MAT

MY WHOLE WORLD CHANGED TODAY!

I went to jiu-jitsu class this afternoon. When I walked onto the mat, there was a new kid there. He looked about my age, maybe a year older, but he was much, much bigger than me. In fact, he was as big if not BIGGER than Kenny Williamson. REALLY BIG.

Doesn't look bigger to me.

Just like other days when new kids show up to class, the instructor pulled the new kid aside and taught him the basics of jiu-jitsu while we were warming up and doing our basic drills for the day. The new kid's name was Jimmy. After warm-up, the instructor sat us down to go over some new moves. We spent some more time drilling those moves, and then, finally, it was time to roll.

I did a round against the usual kids that train all the time. A round with Jeff, a round with Craig, a round with Andy, a round with Nora, and then Dean. Some of them beat me, and I beat some of them. It basically boils down to who has been training the longest or the most. The kid with the most experience will win.

The whole time I was sparring with the other students, Jimmy was standing on the side, watching. Then, after one of the rounds, the instructor said, "Marc, come over here and train with Jimmy, okay?"

I walked over to Jimmy. Now that I was standing near him, I realized how ABSOLUTELY HUGE HE WAS. He was definitely bigger than Kenny Williamson. I held out my hand. Jimmy grabbed my hand and squeezed—not crazy hard like he wanted to hurt me—but he gave it a squeeze, and I could feel how insanely strong he was. I started to get nervous. *What if this big monster goes crazy and tries to hurt me? What if he doesn't know his own strength and ends up breaking my arm or my leg or my SPINE?!*

My nervousness quickly turned to FEAR. I was afraid. I looked at the instructor and said, "Sir, he is A LOT bigger than me. Maybe Jimmy should go with one of the bigger kids?"

The instructor smiled and said, "You'll be fine. Now go ahead and train."

I squared off with Jimmy, we slapped hands, and it was go time.

Still scared, I circled around at a distance, maintaining my focus on Jimmy. Jimmy seemed hesitant, too. He kind of kept looking at me like he was waiting for something to happen. I circled some more. He waited some more. I circled around him EVEN MORE. And he KEPT WAITING.

Then I realized something. The reason Jimmy was waiting was because he had NO IDEA WHAT TO DO. He knew nothing. No single- or double-leg takedowns, no arm locks, no chokes—nothing. He had no idea how to fight.

Now me on the other hand, I was no pro, but I had certainly learned some good stuff over the last six weeks in jiu-jitsu class. That is why the instructor said I would be fine: because he knew that I knew jiu-jitsu.

As I looked at Jimmy's face, my confidence went up, and I decided to go for it.

I reached toward Jimmy's face with my hand to distract him for a moment. His eyes blinked, and he reached up to block my hand. At that moment, I shot in underneath his hands and grabbed both his legs for a double-leg takedown! Almost instantly, I had my arms wrapped around both his legs. I squeezed them together as I pushed him back and to the side with my head. Unable to step back and regain his balance because of my arms around his legs, he began to fall down. He hit the mat, and I immediately got control of him and held him down. He pushed hard against me, but it didn't matter. Even though he was bigger and stronger than I was—it didn't matter. He didn't know any technique—and in jiu-jitsu, technique triumphs over strength and size.

The next thing I did was move into the mount position, and as soon as I did that, Jimmy began to get wild. He bucked his hips and thrashed from side to side and, finally, pushed his arms straight up into my chest to try to get me off him. This is the thing people do when they don't know jiu-jitsu and that's why we drilled it hundreds of times: when someone tries to push you off, they leave their arms wide open to getting arm locked. And that is exactly what I did. In a flash, I spun around, threw my leg over his head, and sat back with his arm under my control. Once I had his arm extended, I squeezed my legs together and slowly raised my hips to apply the tension, and almost instantly, Jimmy tapped out.

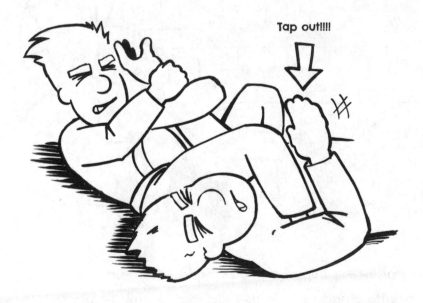

That was it! I had just tapped out a kid bigger than Kenny Williamson! I almost couldn't believe it. I looked at my instructor, who had been watching, and he smiled and nodded at me. Then he gave me a stern look. The stern look was to remind me to stay humble in defeat or victory and to show good sportsmanship and honorable behavior.

I got to my feet, then reached down to Jimmy to help him stand up. I said, "Good job. You are really strong."

He looked disappointed and surprised and said, "Well, it didn't even matter. You are really good at this stuff!"

Stay humble, I thought to myself as I said, "It's just that I have been training longer than you. Don't worry. It's easy to learn, and you'll pick it up fast as long as you keep training."

"Oh, I'm definitely going to keep training. Don't you worry about that."

I wasn't worried at all. In fact, I was happy. Jimmy was nice, but he was also big. That meant I get to train with someone as big as Kenny Williamson ALL THE TIME. The more I train, the more comfortable I will be. So I was happy that Jimmy will keep training. And I WILL, TOO!

CHAPTER 21: SUPER AQUAMAN

Today I learned something that I will never ever forget. Today I learned about fear—and how to beat it.

Ever since I swam across the river on my own, swimming has gotten easier and easier. Uncle Jake has still been taking me to the river every other day, and we have been having a lot of fun—and I have become pretty comfortable in the water. I can swim to the other side and back really easily. I'm relaxed when I'm treading water. I can even swim about halfway across the river completely underwater.

But today I almost forgot about all that comfort. Today I felt fear because today was the day Uncle Jake wanted me to jump off the bridge into the water.

I thought it was going to be just another day of

swimming. We got down to the river, started swimming around, doing what we have been doing. Then Uncle Jake called me over to the sandy little beach by the riverbank. I swam over, kind of showing off my skills!

When I stood up, he said, "Today's the day."

I wasn't quite sure what he was talking about. "What day?" I asked.

"The bridge," he said as he nodded toward the huge bridge that spanned the river.

For some reason—and I can't explain why—I went into panic mode! *THE BRIDGE?!?!* I thought. *THE BRIDGE.* It was tall, and even though I was comfortable in the water, when I thought about jumping from the bridge and landing in the water—I don't know, it just completely FREAKED ME OUT!! So I decided that maybe today wasn't a good day for the bridge, and I tried to make it into No Big Deal.

"I think I'd rather just swim today, Uncle Jake. We can do the bridge jump next time. . . ." As I finished my sentence, I started actually turning around toward the river like I was going to keep swimming.

"Hey!" Uncle Jake said sharply and quickly. I tried to ignore him for another half of a second.

"Hey!" barked Uncle Jake, this time louder and with more force—a force I knew I couldn't ignore anymore. I turned around and faced him.

"You're going off that bridge today," he said in a matter-of-fact way, the way that means Uncle Jake is 100 percent set in his mind, and his mind *will not change*.

But I couldn't help myself from trying to change it anyway. "It's okay, Uncle Jake. I'm just going to swim today. I'll go off the br—"

"It's not okay," Uncle Jake cut me off. "You are going off that bridge. Today."

I knew that arguing was useless. Once Uncle Jake has made up his mind, there is no reasoning with him. And more important, I knew deep inside that he was right. I was ready to jump off the bridge. I was just TERRIFIED!

"Okay, okay, okay," I told Uncle Jake, trying to seem cool about the whole situation as I slowly started walking up the bank of the river toward the bridge.

"I'll watch you from down here," said Uncle Jake.

"Okay," I said softly. I kept walking, and with each step I took, I got more and more terrified about the jump. Time started to slow down. I don't even know why I was so scared—but I was!

Finally, I got to the spot on the bridge where I was supposed to jump. I looked over the edge. HOW DID THE RIVER GET SO FAR DOWN?!?!?!

"Okay! Let's go, Marc," Uncle Jake shouted up to me.

I couldn't even respond. I just stood there.

"Go ahead, Marc. Jump!"

I still couldn't say anything. But I stepped up over the little fence along the side of the bridge and shuffled toward the edge where I was supposed to jump from. I looked straight ahead and was really thinking of doing it. Then I looked down, and I got overwhelmed and scared and I just stood there.

"What's the issue, Marc?!" Uncle Jake yelled up to me.

I didn't know what to say.

"What's wrong?" he asked again, louder.

I just sat there on the little wall along the edge of the bridge.

Then I saw Uncle Jake walking up toward the bridge, obviously coming to either yell at me—or throw me off!!!

But when he got up next to me, he didn't yell at all. Come to think of it, Uncle Jake hardly ever yells.

"What's going on, buddy?" he said in a calm voice.

"I don't know . . . ," I said. "I'm just . . . I'm just . . ."

"You're afraid, aren't you?" Uncle Jake asked. But he wasn't even asking. He knew. He knew I was scared.

There was no point in denying it. Uncle Jake knew it as plain as day.

"Yes," I finally said in a quiet tone, embarrassed that I was afraid.

Then, to my surprise, Uncle Jake said, "That's normal."

"What?" I responded, shocked at Uncle Jake's statement.

"I said, 'That's normal.' You are doing something you've never done before. So it's normal to be a little hesitant. It's called fear. It's a normal emotion—and it's okay." Then he added, "Well, it's okay as long as you can control it."

This made no sense to me. "How am I supposed to control fear? And how would you know? You're not afraid of anything."

Uncle Jake sat quietly for a minute. Then he said, "I wish that were true."

"What do you mean?" I asked him.

"Well, you said I'm not afraid of anything. And that is just not true. Fear is normal. In fact, fear is good. Fear is what warns you when things are dangerous. Fear is what makes you prepare. Fear keeps us out of a lot of trouble. So there is nothing wrong with fear. But fear can also be overwhelming. It can be unreasonable. It can cause you to freeze up and make bad decisions or hesitate when you need to act. So you have to learn to control fear. And that's what you need to do right now."

"Okay. That sounds great, and I would really love to make you happy and overcome my fear . . . but I don't know how!"

Um . . . I'm gonna need you to take a hike.

Uncle Jake thought about what I just asked him for a few seconds and then said, "Okay. Well, the first part of controlling fear you have already done, and that is preparation. You have done plenty of preparation to be ready for this moment—to face this fear. Starting with dunking your head all the way up to swimming all around and back and forth across this river. You have done little jumps off the riverbank. All of the last several weeks have been preparing you for this—this jump. And all that preparation works to help overcome the fear. Imagine how scared you would be if you still didn't know how to swim? You would be horrified. But you have prepared."

"Then why am I still scared?" I asked Uncle Jake.

"Simple," he said. "Because there is still an element of the unknown. You have never jumped off anything this high before. So you don't know what it feels like. People are afraid of what they don't know or they don't understand. But you have prepared. You know it is safe. You know you are ready. It is just this last little bit of fear that has to be overcome. And you know how you do that?"

"I have no idea," I told him.

"You go."

"Just go?" I asked Uncle Jake, now partly thinking he was just joking.

"Yes. You just go. You see, fear lives in the moment—that powerful moment—between when you decide you are going to do something and when you do it. Once you go—once you start—you won't be afraid anymore. You overcome the fear by going—and it is the same in many aspects of life. Parachuting. Talking in front of a crowd. Taking a test. Running a race. Competing in jiu-jitsu. The fear is in the waiting. So. Once you have prepared and trained and studied and planned, there is only one thing left to do: go."

"And that's it?"

"Yes. That's it."

As soon as Uncle Jake finished those words, he stood up, looked at me, yelled out, "HOO-YAH!" and jumped off the bridge.

Just go, I thought to myself. I stood up, stepped up onto the edge of the wall, and looked down at Uncle Jake, who had just come back to the surface and was looking up at me with a big smile on his face.

With all my heart and lungs, I yelled out, "HOO-YAH!!!!" and I stepped off the edge of the bridge, past my fear, and into the unknown. I felt myself falling for a while, and then, *WHOOOOSH*, I was in the water! I came to the surface and had a big smile on my face!

"I can fly!" I yelled. "I can flyyyyyyyyyy!!!"

Uncle Jake laughed and got out and ran up and jumped again, and I followed him—without hesitation. And then we did it again and again and again. And the fear? It was gone. All I had to do was prepare and get ready and then . . . I just had to take the first step—GO!

CHAPTER 22: TEN!

I never thought that this day would come. Uncle Jake
had me rest for two straight days in the morning
instead of working out. The first morning instead of
working out, he took me to breakfast. The next day
we ate breakfast at home, and he started teaching
me how to play chess—which seems like a really
complicated game but is actually pretty easy once you
understand it.

Then, after two days of rest, Uncle Jake met me
down in the garage in the morning to work out.

"Today is the big day," he said.

"Why is that?" I asked.

"You will see," said Uncle Jake. "Now, get up on the pull-up bar and do one pull-up."

"One?" I asked, not believing that Uncle Jake would only have me do *one* pull-up.

"Yes—just one," Uncle Jake replied.

I jumped up on the bar and did a pull-up. I was a little stiff, but it did feel pretty easy.

"Now another one," Uncle Jake ordered.

"Just one?" I asked.

"Yes—just one."

I grabbed ahold of the pull-up bar and pulled my chin over the bar. Now a little warmer, I felt even stronger. Then Uncle Jake had me do one more and then one more and then one more. As I got warmer and warmer and more loosened up, I felt stronger and stronger. Then Uncle Jake said, "Now you are going to rest for about two minutes." I stretched my arms a little and waited for the time to go by. Then Uncle Jake said, "Now. Jump up on the bar and do ten pull-ups."

I should have known this was coming. But the weird thing was, instead of being concerned that I wouldn't be able to do it, I felt really strong and like I *actually* could do it. "Okay," I said.

I stepped up and grabbed a tight hold of the pull-up bar. Uncle Jake said, "Go," and I started pulling.

One. Two. Three. Four. I wasn't even feeling these yet. Five. Six. Seven. I felt a little tired but not too bad. And I was about to break my record! Eight. There were eight pull-ups. The most I've ever done IN MY LIFE. And I wasn't done yet. I pulled again. NINE. Yes! Another record. I was a little tired, but I knew I had another one in me. So I pulled again and got my chin over the bar. "Ten!" Uncle Jake said. I dropped off the bar. And then I jumped into the air.

"I did it!" I yelled, and then quickly corrected what I had said: "*WE* did it!"

Uncle Jake gave me a high five and then said, "No, that wasn't us. It was you. I might have told you what to do, but make no mistake: You did this."

"Well, I couldn't have done it without you, Uncle Jake," I told him.

"Maybe so. But you did the work. You did the practice. You did the pull-ups. Well done, Marc," he told me. And then he added, "Now get up there and do another set of ten."

And I did just that! I jumped up on the bar and was able to do another ten pull-ups. And then I did another set of ten and then a set of nine and then two sets of eight, a set of seven, four sets of six, two sets of five, two sets of four, then three, two, and one.

And that was it! I was now officially a kid who can do TEN pull-ups. No more hiding from the pull-up bar in school. No more being embarrassed about being weak. This was real. As I thought about this, I looked at Uncle Jake and said, "Thanks."

"No problem, Marc. And I want you to remember something: This isn't just about pull-ups. You know what else this is about?"

I wasn't quite sure. "I don't know."

Uncle Jake grabbed me by both shoulders and looked me straight in the eyes and said gravely,

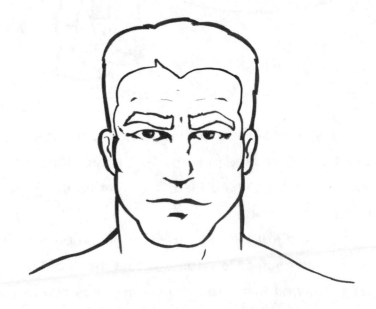

"This is about *everything*. Everything. Just think, two months ago, you couldn't do any pull-ups. At all. Zero. Now you can do TEN. All it took was a good plan and the discipline to execute the plan. To DO IT. That's what it takes. And you can apply that to just about anything. If you are willing to do the work—you can *make things happen*. And like I told you, no one else is going to do the work for you. Sure, you might get some help along the way. But you might not. Who knows? What we do know is this: Hard work and discipline are how you achieve things. You have to *make things happen*. And that is exactly what you did here, and what you can do with almost anything in life. Remember that."

"I will, Uncle Jake. I will," I told him. And he was 100 percent right. People say you can do anything you want in life. But what they don't tell you is that you have to work for it.

With hard work, anything is possible.

CHAPTER 23: STAND ALONE

It didn't even hit me until last night when I saw Uncle Jake packing up all his gear that he was leaving. Just like that, summer was over, and just like that, Uncle Jake was leaving. I must have looked pretty sad, because Uncle Jake asked me what was wrong.

"What's wrong? You're leaving, that's what's wrong."

"Yeah, but you're going back to school, and you will be back with all your buddies."

"I know but . . ." I tried to think of a way to say what I was thinking.

"But what?" Uncle Jake asked.

"But none of those kids can help me be strong. None of those kids can teach me to do things I don't know how to do. None of those kids are warriors, like you."

Sorry, Fred. You're just not a warrior.

I know. Can you help me get out of this sack?

"Hmmm," Uncle Jake mumbled. I thought for the first time that Uncle Jake was stumped.

"How am I going to keep getting stronger and smarter and better without you around? How am I going to be a warrior all by myself?"

Uncle Jake took a hard look at me; then he said, "The truth is, you don't need me around to be a warrior. Oftentimes, the warrior stands alone. It can happen for many reasons. Maybe he got left behind. Maybe the rest of his team got killed. Maybe he just grew old, and his fellow warriors died. Maybe he got assigned a job that put him out there, on the battlefield, by himself. None of that matters. The warrior remains strong. The warrior must know how to stand alone."

Only my uncle Jake could make being left by myself sound cool! But I still wasn't buying it. "Okay, but who is going to train me and help me study? Who is going to make sure I get up in the morning? Who is going to make sure I don't go back to my old lazy ways?"

Uncle Jake answered quickly, "You don't need me for that anymore. As a matter of fact, you never needed me. Sure, I showed you the path, but you could have found it on your own. You know what you need to do to stay on the warrior path. Hard work. Discipline.

Study. Eat good food. Keep your room and your gear in order. Set new goals and work hard to meet them. Keep training jiu-jitsu. This is all stuff you know. As a matter of fact, this is all stuff you can actually teach and share with your friends. And you need to do that. You need to become a leader—to help your friends learn to be stronger and smarter and better. Teach them to be the best they can be. You have changed a lot over the summer. The other kids will see that. You will become a leader now. They will follow."

"I'm not sure I'm ready to be a leader," I told Uncle Jake, thinking about what that would be like.

"People usually don't feel like they are ready to be leaders. But I am telling you, you are ready.

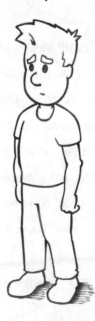

"You know the path. And you are humble. That is the most important thing about being a leader. Remember that you don't know everything. Listen and take advice from other people. Always be ready to learn and try to be better. Those are qualities a leader needs, and you have them. Trust me, Marc. You're going to have a great year at school."

With that, Uncle Jake went back to packing up all his gear, and the next morning, my mom and I drove him to the airport. When we got there I was feeling sad and wasn't saying much. We pulled up to the airport and stopped next to the curb to drop off Uncle Jake.

I got out of the car to say good-bye.

My mom got out, too. She hugged Uncle Jake, and then she looked at him and said, "Thank you. For everything," and after she said *everything* she looked right at me. Even my mom noticed how much Uncle Jake had helped me.

He gave me a hug, then reached into his bag and pulled out a little box and gave it to me. "This is for you, Warrior Kid." He held out his hand for a shake. I gripped it and gave it a good squeeze. "Better," he said. "But you still have work to do on that grip." Then, just like that, he turned and walked away.

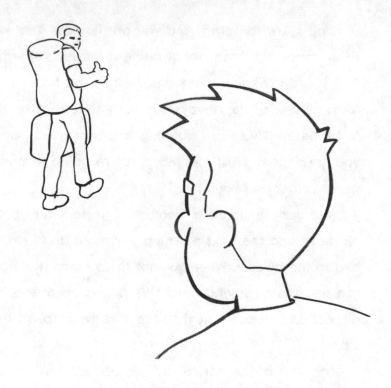

I felt sad, but I actually didn't feel as sad as I thought I would. I opened the box. In it was a watch, just like Uncle Jake had, and on the watchband was a little compass that pointed north. There was a little note inside the box from Uncle Jake. It said *The watch will help you stay disciplined by making you remember to get better every second of the day. I already set the alarm for early morning every day. The compass will remind you to stay on the warrior path. Discipline Equals Freedom. Uncle Jake.*

I put the watch on, and I don't think I will ever take it off.

CHAPTER 24: FIRST DAYS BACK TO SCHOOL

Well, the first day of sixth grade was A LOT different from my last day of fifth grade. It was AWESOME! Where do I begin?

It all started in my math class. We had to take a timed test on the multiplication tables. We had fifteen minutes to do it. I was done in six minutes. And when I got done I went back and checked every answer. I knew them all 100 percent!

8 x 8 = 64
7 x 9 = 63
4 x 6 = 24
5 x 5 = 25
3 x 9 = 27

Right before recess, we had a "fitness baseline test" where we had to do two minutes' worth of push-ups, two minutes of sit-ups, and, of course, one set of as many pull-ups as we could do. I did eighty-two push-ups, ninety-one sit-ups, and FOURTEEN PULL-UPS! Only

one kid in my class did more than me, Taylor, who
is super strong and did sixteen. But it was awesome.
There were a couple of kids that remembered last year
when I couldn't do any. They were watching like hawks
when I walked over to the bar, and I know they were
waiting to make fun of me.

Instead, when I got done (beating both of them, by
the way!), they asked how I did so many. I answered
them in one word: "Practice."

Soon after, the recess bell rang, and all the kids
flooded the playground. I made my way over to the

jungle gym. Of course, Kenny Williamson was there. The first day of school and he was already bullying people and not letting them on the jungle gym. It was just him and a few of his so-called friends hanging out there. A couple other kids were hanging around the border of the jungle gym, scared to go on it.

I wasn't scared. I walked right over to it and up the stairs to the platform that leads to the monkey bars. I swung across the monkey bars, and when I got to the other side and dropped down, Kenny was standing and looking at me.

"What do you think you are doing, Marc?" he growled at me.

I acted really innocent. "Me? I'm going on the monkey bars," I told him.

"You can't go on the monkey bars. Those are my monkey bars. In fact, you can't go on the jungle gym at all—THIS IS MY JUNGLE GYM," Kenny said sternly as he stepped a little closer to me.

"This isn't your jungle gym, Kenny. This is everyone's jungle gym," I responded in a calm voice.

I could tell this surprised Kenny. No one had ever questioned him before. He didn't like it and told me, "NO, IT ISN'T. This jungle gym is MINE. I am the king of the jungle gym." A few other kids started to gather around to watch.

"No, Kenny. You are not the king of the jungle gym. Not anymore," I told him. The other kids looked shocked at what I had said.

"You will see who the king is after I smash your little face," Kenny said to me as he brought his hand up and closed his fingers into a fist. There were even more kids watching now, and you could hear a pin drop as everyone expected me to get crushed.

Then I got really serious. Super serious. The most serious I have ever been in my whole life. I had never felt this way before. I wasn't angry, and I wasn't even mad. But I was ready. All the training, all the jiu-jitsu, all the wrestling and sparring and pull-ups and working out. I knew 100 percent I was going to beat him. I stepped even closer to Kenny and said, "Go ahead and try, and I promise that you will never forget what I do to you."

I was even a little surprised those words came out of my mouth. And it certainly surprised Kenny, too. I saw something change in his eyes. With all the training and sparring I had done, I now knew for sure that I could beat him in a fight—and now it seemed like he knew that, too. And I realized that in all those years of being bigger and stronger and meaner than all the other kids, no one had ever stood up to him—and he had never actually been in a fight. All of a sudden, he was scared. He put his hand down. He stepped back. He looked down at the ground and walked away.

The crowd of kids let out a sigh. I turned around and jumped back on the monkey bars and made it back to the platform. I climbed to the next level. The other kids were all just standing there, looking at me. I waved my hands and told them to come on up. One kid did. And then another, and then another. Before long, kids were all over the jungle gym, playing, running, swinging. It was great.

Except Kenny. He was sitting by himself with his head hung low. Even the kids that usually followed him around were gone. Then I remembered one of the things I learned in jiu-jitsu and one of the things Uncle Jake taught me: Treat other people with respect. So I walked over to Kenny and said, "Hey, Kenny."

He looked up at me and said, "Yeah?"

"The jungle gym is for everyone. 'Everyone' includes you. Come on." I motioned with my head toward the jungle gym and turned and walked back toward it. After a few steps, I looked over my shoulder. Kenny was still sitting down, looking at me. I waved him over again. He didn't move. So I smiled and waved him over again. He cracked a little smile, stood up, and started walking toward me. When he got close enough, I said, "I'll race you to the monkey bars."

He stood with a surprised look on his face until I said, "GO!" and we both started running.

He barely beat me there, and when I got to the top, he held up his hand for a high five.

Just like that, Kenny wasn't the king anymore. And he also wasn't a bully. Soon he was laughing and playing with the rest of the kids—he was now one of the kids.

It was only the first day of school, but I could tell this year was going to be the best year ever.

CHAPTER 25: LETTER TO UNCLE JAKE

Uncle Jake has been gone for about two weeks now. I miss having him around, but I am still staying on the warrior path even without him here. I wrote him this letter to thank him for everything he did for me.

Uncle Jake,

I hope you are having a good time at college. I can tell you I am having THE BEST time at school EVER. I have aced all my math tests. I did FOURTEEN pull-ups during the first test in gym class. The trip to Mount Tom was AMAZING. I can't believe

I couldn't swim before! And finally, I stood up to Kenny Williamson—and when I did, he backed down. He no longer controls the jungle gym. ALL OF THIS is because of YOU. Thank you for showing me the Way of the Warrior Kid. I don't know how I can ever thank you for everything you did for me. So I guess for now, I will just say thank you.

Also, you told me I should have my own Warrior Kid Code. Here it is:

1. The Warrior Kid wakes up early in the morning.
2. The Warrior Kid studies to learn and gain knowledge and asks questions if he doesn't understand.
3. The Warrior Kid trains hard, exercises, and eats right to be strong and fast and healthy.
4. The Warrior Kid trains to know how to fight so he can stand up to bullies to protect the weak.
5. The Warrior Kid treats people with respect and helps out other people whenever possible.
6. The Warrior Kid keeps things neat and is always prepared and ready for action.

7. The Warrior Kid stays humble.

8. The Warrior Kid works hard and always does his best.

9. I am the Warrior Kid.

And that is it, Uncle Jake. That is my Warrior Kid Code. Let me know if there is anything I should add or take away. Or anything else I should do.

Just like the Navy SEALs have their Trident symbol and the Rangers have their Ranger Tab and the Marines have their Eagle, Globe, and Anchor symbol, I made up a symbol that means WARRIOR KID. It will always remind me who I am. Here it is.

One more thing that has happened since school started. Some of the other kids, especially ones that remember how pathetic I was last year, have been asking what I did to get stronger and smarter and tougher. I have told them about everything you taught me. I am teaching them how to work out and how to use flash cards and how to study and I have even shown them some basic jiu-jitsu moves. And they are listening to me. It is almost like I am the leader of the group. But don't worry, I am staying humble. I'll tell you more about that later.

Anyway. Again, thanks for everything, Uncle Jake. Thanks for making me stronger and faster and smarter and better. Thanks for taking me to jiu-jitsu so I won't get picked on and so I can stick up for others. Thanks for turning me into a Warrior Kid.

> With thanks, respect, and love,
> Your nephew,
> Marc

And that was it. I was lucky to have Uncle Jake. But not everyone has an Uncle Jake. I know that. I also know that it doesn't really matter. Uncle Jake showed me the Way of the Warrior Kid, but the Way isn't magic. There aren't any tricks. You don't need someone to lead you down the path. You can walk down the path by yourself: Wake up early. Exercise hard. Eat good food. Study. Train jiu-jitsu. The path to being a Warrior Kid is simple—but it is not easy. Sometimes it is hard to wake up early in the morning. Sometimes you won't want to work out. Sometimes it is hard to go train jiu-jitsu. Sometimes you want to eat junk food! And in all those situations, that is when you have to use discipline to MAKE YOURSELF STAY ON THE PATH. In the long run, the path of discipline will set you free. . . .